Brilliant.
Pacy, thrilling and authentic,
The Settlement *has all the ingredients of a perfect novel. A must read.*

DAME FIONA REYNOLDS – MASTER EMMANUEL COLLEGE CAMBRIDGE.

I love it!
Wonderful compelling story so well told. The location, events and relationships are evoked so vividly.

PROFESSOR INGRID DAY – ADELAIDE AUSTRALIA.

An absolute corker.

KAREN HOLMES – EDITOR AND AUTHOR.

First Edition published 2021 by

2QT Limited (Publishing)
Settle, North Yorkshire BD24 9RH United Kingdom

Cover Design by Charlotte Mouncey

Printed in Great Britain by Ingram Sparks

A CIP catalogue record for this book is available
from the British Library
ISBN 978-1-913071-99-8

BACKGROUND

Jim and Tom

My father used to entertain us with stories of his childhood and youth. He was allowed to run wild and was totally spoilt by a bevy of loving foster sisters. He was the scallywag, the rapscallion, the miscreant until he was finally tamed by my mother. It was only when he died that I began to consider the stories he had told us and to look more deeply into his history.

Much of it was true and it is told in chapters three and four of the book as Jim's story. The letters which form part of the text, those of Sally, Jim, and the anonymous letter, are all real and are in my possession. The rest of the book is fiction.

My father was born in August 1919 and went to his grave thinking he was illegitimate – a much bigger issue for those of his generation than for us today. I did some research and found that his parents were married by special licence in April 1919, so he was not illegitimate – but only just.

His biological parents lived in Co Armagh in a village close to the border with Co Monaghan. This county line became the border between the two new states of Ireland, north and south, in 1921. I began to wonder about what life was like for my grandparents during that time. The decade 1910–1920 was full of political unrest with forces in Ireland agitating for independence and those in Ulster equally adamant they wished to remain part of the United Kingdom. Research revealed a rich and interesting period of history. There was a story to be told.

My main source for historical information was the book – 'A History of Ulster' by Jonathan Bardon. It was only when I read his biographical notes that I realised I had socialised in the same group as him, briefly, during my first year at Queen's. Small world – but so typical of Northern Ireland.

THE SETTLEMENT

RUTH KIRBY-SMITH

I would like to dedicate the book to my grandchildren
KATJA, SKYLA, ISOLA AND AUGUST.

Chapter 1

BACK TO LINDARA

Olivia, 1984

'Sorry for your trouble. Sorry for your trouble.'

The words flowed over Olivia like a balm. She found the old-fashioned phrase curiously comforting. It served these country folks well, giving words to those too shy or tongue-tied to know what to say in the face of death, giving comfort to the family in the rawness of bereavement. Did they have an equivalent in Boston? She had lived there for five years but her American friends and family were young and healthy, leading full, productive lives, so she had yet to experience death in America.

She moved slowly through the small crowd of mourners standing in the spring sunshine, shaking a hand, remembering a face, or introducing herself as Sarah's granddaughter to those she did not know.

'Ah now, she had a good innings,' she heard more than once.

'Yes, she did,' Olivia replied. What else could you say about someone who had died peacefully in bed at the age of ninety-two? In the midst of the bombings and shootings in Northern Ireland, it was a blessing.

She looked across the garden to the road winding up over the bridge, past the gates of the Clanhugh estate, and into the village. She tried to put this morning's incident out of her mind, but it kept coming back to her. What was the meaning of it? Why would someone want to do such a thing at the funeral of an old woman? She stood quietly, a little apart, taking in the serenity of the spring-draped countryside.

This place lay at the prime meridian of her heart. Sometimes at home in Boston she found herself looking along the Charles River, visualising this green valley beyond the ocean. She thought of her friends and family, her haunts in the city, her university days – but her thoughts always came back to this lush wooded valley on the River Blackwater. It was the Eden of her childhood.

There had never been any trouble in Lindara. Summers there were idyllic, full of freedom. She would roam the woods with a gang of children, fishing in the river, making dens, playing hide-and-seek. There were none of the restrictions of the city. Each year she slotted back into the local gang, where the son of Lord Clanhugh played with the gamekeeper's boys, and even Bobby, who was disabled, was included in the fun. In her memory the grown-ups were the same – working together, playing football, drinking in the village pub without any feuding or bitterness.

In all the years of the Troubles there had never been strife in Lindara, but was it the perfect place of her memory? If so, how could she explain the look of pure hatred on the face of the man who insulted her grandmother in her coffin?

She had felt a sense of unease as soon as she'd climbed into the funeral car that morning. There she sat with her mother and father, looking straight ahead as they followed the hearse. All she could look at was the oak coffin surrounded by flowers. It was then that the finality of it hit her, and her eyes stung with tears at the thought of losing her grandmother forever. She felt trapped, as if she were in a black tunnel, and she passed over the bridge and went past the gates of the estate feeling raw with grief.

As the procession entered the village, she tore her eyes from the coffin and looked out. Lindara was a beautiful place. The architecture was classic Georgian, built in beige sandstone, with flame-coloured ivy adding the final touch of elegance to the buildings in the main street. It had been the brainchild of the original Lord Clanhugh, after he was granted the thousand acres straddling the counties of Armagh and Monaghan on which he built his country seat and the model village at its gates. She had always appreciated the beauty of Lindara, yet for the first time the cold formality of the village struck her in its contrast to the pretty colonial houses of the Boston suburbs.

This culture shock swamped her each time she crossed the Atlantic. But then, within a few days, she adjusted. On her first trip to America she had worked the summer season in a seaside resort on the New Jersey shore. She was amazed by the brashness of it all – the motels with names like Shangri-La flashing bright neon lights, the boardwalk with foods she had never heard of. Saltwater taffy, root beer, thirty different kinds of ice cream, waffles and maple syrup for breakfast, acres of rides on the seafront.

The people came in every shape and size too. Fat old ladies wore shorts and sloppy T-shirts in gaudy colours that would have been unthinkable in Ireland.

'Can they see themselves?' she wondered. 'Do they realise how outrageous they look?' Yet, when she returned home, she could not believe how drab the Irish looked in their sensible grey and beige. After three months in America, Ireland seemed a buttoned-up, cheerless place. Though she had lived in Boston for five years she always needed to make this mental adjustment when she travelled back and forth.

That morning she had noticed the man as soon as their car slowed to turn right to the church. He was leaning against the wall with his back to the funeral cortège, but he slowly turned as the hearse eased around the corner and raised himself to his full height. He was tall, with a muscular build, and he was much older than Olivia had first guessed. His eyes never left the hearse as he moved with a long, slow stride through the crowd to the edge of the pavement. No one seemed to be aware of him except her, but she could not take her eyes off him. It was the look on his face and the proud way he held himself that made her skin prickle.

He stood at the edge of the pavement, exactly on the corner, a full head higher than those around him. Olivia waited for him to dip his head as a sign of respect, but he stood there, very still, his hard blue eyes fixed on the oak coffin. Then he stepped forward and it seemed for a moment that he wanted to touch the coffin, to make the last contact with her grandmother before she was buried. Slowly, he lifted his head back, looking to the sky, then he jerked forward and spat a long stream down the window of the hearse.

She could not hear the words he said, but she did not need to hear them to know that he had cursed her grandmother with a heart full of hate. There was a low gasp and the villagers around him looked away in embarrassment. He paused for a moment, turned, and then, like the parting of the Red Sea, the crowd stepped to one side as he moved swiftly between them and disappeared from view.

***

The man's name was on everyone's lips as they gathered at the house to pay their respects. The tall figure, who had strolled towards the hearse and then so publicly disrespected her grandmother, was called Michael O'Connell.

'Aw, sure, them O'Connells were always the same. Nothing but a shower of hooligans. There was always hard feeling between Sarah and that lot.' Olivia was told this more than once, but no one seemed to know why there was animosity between them. It was just there, and always had been, as long as anyone could remember.

She recalled two families in the village by that name, but they had never been close friends of the children she'd played with when she came to stay. They were older and did not want to be bothered with the younger kids. One thing she did remember about them was that the O'Connells were either red-haired, freckled and gawky, or dark-haired, blue-eyed and beautiful. There was no in-between. She tried to recollect if her grandmother had ever mentioned the O'Connells, but she could not think of a single link between her and them over the years.

When the last stragglers were leaving, she wandered down to the bridge over the Blackwater. She could not get the image of the man out of her mind. Over and over again she saw him, as if in a flickering, black-and-white movie – leaning back, looking upward, and then jerking forward as the long stream of spit hit the side of the hearse. She could see the arc of it hang in the air, an innocent stream of water until it landed beside the coffin, as a curse.

Why would he do it? She asked herself the question a hundred times, wondering what could make a normal human being behave like that. What would drive him to make such a public statement of hatred? Surely no one could feel such venom towards her grandmother, who was well liked and respected in the village?

If Olivia had to catch the essence of her grandmother in one word it would be *Lady*. She could picture her tall, lean figure walking up the aisle in church to the front pew, alongside the one occupied by the Clanhughs when they were at home. Her steely grey hair was always knotted high on the back of her head in a bun and covered with a wide-brimmed hat, and her suit was always a classic cut in a subdued colour. The wardrobe in her bedroom was full of clothes, some from the couture houses of Paris, that hadn't been worn for years.

Sarah was a regular churchgoer, but she shied away from social commitments. Her only contribution to the church, apart from her money, was the annual garden party. Even then, Olivia knew that tolerating people trekking through her garden was as much as she could bear. On the whole, Sarah lived the life of a recluse.

As Olivia watched the waters rippling past the dark green weed, the question shifted in her mind to what Sarah had done to cause such strong feelings. She loved her grandmother dearly, had never had any cause to dislike or question her, yet, as she pondered, the distance created by five years abroad allowed questions and doubts to surface. Like tilting a kaleidoscope, Olivia began to glimpse a new and different view.

It was ironic that she, who had spent her career in scientific research – asking questions, never accepting the obvious – should take so long to question the integrity of her grandmother. But then she was bound by love, emotion, kinship and all the things that were a hindrance to objective inquiry. Olivia knew that, to get to the bottom of today's events, she would have to start looking at her grandmother's life with an unbiased eye.

She began to think about the quirks of her grandmother's character. Her house was her pride, but her garden was her passion. She was out of doors in all weathers in old clothes and boots, weeding, planting and pruning. The Colonel – a thin, toothless wire of a man – worked by her side five days a week. They squabbled like children over the ideal potting mix or the position of a plant and then, once the altercation was over, they would sit in the summerhouse drinking tea and chatting. Every afternoon, the Colonel offered Sarah a cigarette and she accepted. On winter afternoons they always added a nip of Bushmills to each cup.

The Colonel had been the gardener for Sarah for as long as Olivia could remember, and she recalled how amused she was, as a child, when she realised that the Colonel was not a kernel. That hard, brown-eyed little man had always been a nut encasing a soft, sweet interior in her childhood mind, but now she realised that thinking such a rough old rogue could have been a colonel in the British army was even more ridiculous.

Was there ever more than just friendship between them?

She knew without a doubt that there was not, yet there was never the simple mistress and employee relationship either. It was something more complex, that only the two of them understood. Swearing was like breathing to the Colonel, but Sarah seemed indifferent to it except when Olivia was there.

'Whist, Colonel, the child is here. Watch your language,' her grandmother would say, but it was useless. Swearing ran through the Colonel's language like yeast in bread.

She clearly remembered one perfect spring day. She was busy damming the stream at the bottom of the garden, while Grandmother had the minister's wife and two of the ladies from the church to tea. They were in the green sitting room, discussing the arrangements for the annual garden party, with the French windows open to the garden. The Colonel was muttering to himself and swearing under his breath. Olivia watched him, wondering what on earth was eating him that day.

As the meeting went on he grew restless and made a point of walking past the open windows, looking in, impatient for the meeting to end. Eventually, he moved closer and started weeding the garden bed beside the windows. When there was a lull in the conversation, the ladies clearly heard him say,

'There she is sitting in there on her fat arse instead of out here doing a decent day's work.' There was an embarrassed silence, and then the ladies cleared their throats, drank their tea and left.

Olivia waited, wondering what her grandmother would say, making sure to stay well out of the way near the stream but close enough to hear what was going on. The Colonel hummed to himself and whistled out of tune, noticeably happier now that they had gone.

When Sarah appeared in her old clothes, she put her hands on her hips, fixed the wiry figure with a hard stare and said,

'What are we going to do with you, Colonel?' Olivia remembered skulking closer, waiting for the row to start, but next thing she knew they were doubled up, howling with laughter.

It wasn't so strange to have a public and a private persona, it was just that Sarah's private persona was so different from her public one. Olivia loved her grandmother for that, loved the fact that she had a mischievous and devil-may-care side to her character.

Still staring into the water, Olivia realised how little she really understood of Sarah's life. She knew that she had married a wealthy widower in his sixties when she was a teenager, and that after he'd died she married John Brown. With him she had a son – Olivia's father – who was raised by a foster family because Sarah and John were busy working in the business. She also knew there was a stepson from Sarah's first marriage, who had gone to England many years ago. The family only found out about him after he died because Sarah was the executor of his will.

Standing on the bridge, she had a pure adult moment. Looking back at the official version of her family history, none of it rang true. As a child, she had accepted everything she was told, but now her mind was full of questions. Did she really know her grandmother? Each time she tried to define her, she thought of a contradictory fact that was equally true. She was a lady, yet she could be earthy and even coarse at times. She was a loving anchor for the family, yet she had paid a foster family to raise her only son. She had married two wealthy men, yet had apparently ignored the existence of a stepson for years. She lived a simple, open life, but there were corners of it hidden and never explained.

The most serious case to answer was the way she had treated Olivia's father, Jim. It was all family history now, and the rift between them had been healed, but she knew her father was scarred in some deep, permanent way where his mother was concerned.

Jim was born on a summer day in the seaside town of Rostrevor, where Sarah had gone on holiday. When he was three days old, two sisters from a family at the Spa came in a pony and trap to collect him. They took him to his foster home, where he was brought up by the family until, at the age of ten, his father and mother came to reclaim him.

As a child, Olivia had often heard the story of how he came back with them in a big black car to a house that had the best of everything. Carpets, fancy furniture, electric lights in every room, inside bathrooms, and a garage with two cars and an array of tools that made his eyes shine. He lived with them for the whole of that long summer and started at school in Armagh in September, but he missed his foster family and all his friends. Sarah and John were his biological mother and father, but he said they were like strangers to him. Her father had told her he was so desperately unhappy and homesick that he'd written to the two oldest girls at the Spa, and they had hatched a plan to take him back.

Apparently, he did not see his mother again until he was nineteen, when he rode his motorbike to Lindara and arrived on her doorstep. He said that when she opened the door she did not recognise him and asked him what he wanted. He'd had to tell his mother who he was. Olivia could only imagine how that must have felt. Over the years they had managed to rebuild their relationship, and the bond between Jim and Sarah was undoubtedly strengthened by the closeness that had grown between Olivia and her grandmother. It was never acknowledged that the time – and love – that Sarah lavished on Olivia was her way of compensating, but at heart all the family knew it.

Olivia relished the quirkiness of her father's family history, so different from her mother's normal family life. She loved the stories he told of his unusual childhood – yet, when she asked her grandmother, she never had much to say about any of it. She did not avoid the subject, but she always gave just the bare bones of a story. She was different, though, when she talked about John. Her eyes lit up and she retreated into some private world of her own, and she would sigh and say,

'Aw, sure, there was nobody like him.'

Now, as Olivia reviewed the facts in her mind, the truth hit her. Why would her grandmother go on a holiday to Rostrevor, which was miles away, just weeks before she was due to give birth? Why would she give a three-day-old baby to a family from the Spa, a hamlet thirty miles in the other direction and even further from home?

One explanation, though simple, had never occurred to her before.

Her father was illegitimate.

CHAPTER 2

SARAH'S HOUSE

OLIVIA, 1984

In her years as a student in Belfast, Olivia had learnt the principles and details of biochemistry, and she had also learnt the language of war. While studying in the university library, Olivia had felt the glass in the large windows resonate on many occasions as a bomb went off somewhere in the city. The echo of it would bounce between the hills to the north and the south, exaggerating the boom of the explosion. She had seen, many times, the grey smoke rising from the city centre, and had known that some landmark that had survived untouched for years had been destroyed in an instant. Often the smoke would turn black, which was a sign that a major fire was now raging.

She had learnt to read the sounds of war, as gun battles raged during the hours of darkness – ra-ta-ta-tat, ra-ta-ta-tat, boom, kaboom – and then the eey-aww, eey-aww of the ambulance, the clang of a fire engine bell. She would lie uneasily in her bed in the university area, knowing she was never completely safe.

In the end Olivia had made a decision to leave – as much out of frustration with the violence and hatred that seemed to have no end as the fact that she had fallen in love with an American. Even if that had not happened, she knew she would not have stayed in Ireland to watch it being torn apart. She had been glad to leave, and only weddings and funerals would ever be able to draw her back. Olivia thought of her grandmother, who had remained in Ireland all her life. With her money, she could have chosen to live anywhere, but instead she had always stayed in Lindara.

Olivia was back at her grandmother's house after the funeral. The house was as it had always been, furnished with good-quality mahogany items and decorated with silver ornaments and Persian rugs. Today, it was quiet and still, perhaps a little more faded and dusty than before, but otherwise just as she always pictured it in her vivid memories of childhood.

Olivia wanted to visit the house while she was there, as she wasn't sure when she might next be back in Northern Ireland. She was keen to soak in its atmosphere one more time – and she also wanted to look for anything that could shed light on the mystery of the man at the funeral. She had been racking her brain for any details she could recall from her grandmother's life that might provide an explanation.

She did remember one strange event. In 1978, a letter had arrived from a solicitor in Cambridge notifying Sarah of the death of one Mr S. Orr, and listing her as his sole executor. It turned out to be Sarah's stepson, Samuel, who had not been heard of for decades. Sarah had rarely mentioned him, so they had assumed he was long dead. Yet, when the news came, Sarah seemed strangely unmoved. It was as if she had been expecting it.

It was only then that she talked about Samuel. He was twelve years old when Sarah, a teenager herself, had married his father. To Sarah, he was always more like a brother than a stepson. He helped with the family business during the war and afterwards went to London to train as an accountant. Sometime later he moved to Cambridge, became the bursar at one of the colleges and stayed there for the rest of his life.

The facts of the story were straightforward enough, but Olivia was never fully satisfied with Sarah's explanations. She wondered why Samuel hadn't come back and taken over the business when it was so successful. Surely her first husband would have wanted his son, his own flesh and blood, to inherit the business rather than his wife? Had Sarah cheated Samuel out of his inheritance? Lindara was a thriving commercial village when Samuel lived there, and the mill provided employment for all the villages around. They worked day and night during the war, weaving linen for uniforms, stretchers and tents, and making Blackwater Mills highly profitable.

Why had Samuel not been in touch with the family for all those years? If he had contacted Sarah, why did she never mention him? If there had been a misunderstanding between them, would he have chosen Sarah to be his executor? It was one more instance of Sarah's explanations making logical sense but somehow not giving the full story. It seemed as if the essential parts had been carefully edited out.

Strangest of all, though, was that the final twist in the Samuel story had surprised even Sarah. She said she had been completely flummoxed by it. Samuel Orr, formerly known as Samuel Grey, had left half of his estate, worth a quarter of a million pounds, to a Catholic man, who had no known connection to the family.

Olivia had decided to visit Cambridge, the city where Samuel had lived, in the summer of 1978, immediately after her finals at Queen's University. Samuel's death and the money left to the unknown man had intrigued her, and she had been determined to find out more about the man who would have been her uncle, had she ever got to know him. Olivia had a school friend studying at Magdalene College and she had arranged to stay with her. Her grandmother had given her Samuel's old address and his college details, and had seemed happy that Olivia was making the trip.

Like millions of visitors before her, she had been bewitched by the beauty of the city, awestruck by the architecture and seduced by the delights of the ancient libraries and punting on the Cam. As she had sat on the banks of the river taking in the atmosphere of the city, she had compared her student life in Belfast with that of her friend there. Olivia knew she was seeing Cambridge at its best, in the warmth and sunshine of an English summer, but it contrasted starkly with the grey winter months of rain and drizzle that were characteristic of Belfast.

After contacting Samuel's old college, Olivia had been put in touch with a close friend of her step-uncle, who had agreed to meet her for lunch and tell her about Samuel's life. They had met at the front of King's College and walked past The Senate House, down the cobbled lane to a small entrance, and had then climbed the granite stairs, curved with wear, to the senior common room. The long room where lunch was being served was furnished with low tables, Persian carpets and overstuffed couches. One ancient professor was asleep in an armchair and she could have sworn that, in the diffuse light from the high window, she had seen the fine gossamer of a spider's web attached to him. She'd felt honoured to be treated to lunch in the inner sanctum of the ancient university and had found Samuel's friend, Geoffrey, also from Northern Ireland, charming company.

Over lunch he had talked with great fondness of Samuel, who had been his friend for over forty years.

'Ah, sure, he was a great chap. He was kind, decent and intelligent, and the best company a man could wish for. We became friends right from the start when he moved to Cambridge, as we were both Ulstermen and both of us had a love of fishing.'

'I am so sorry I never got to know him. I think we would have hit it off.'

'Samuel got on with everyone. You will not find anyone to say a bad word about him.'

'It seems he never married. Did he have someone in his life?'

'Oh, he had a number of partners over the years because he was very attractive to the ladies, but somehow he just seemed to prefer his own space and company. My wife tried to match him up numerous times but it never came to anything. He was very content with his life as a bachelor.'

'There is one other thing I want to ask you about. Did you always know him as Samuel Orr or did he ever use the name Grey? It may seem strange, but he actually changed his name at some stage when he came to live in England.'

Samuel's friend sat back on his seat and looked at Olivia in surprise.

'No, I never heard anything of the sort. I had no idea he'd changed his name. He certainly was Samuel Orr for all his time in Cambridge, and that was forty-odd years.'

'My parents and I don't know why he changed his name, either. Maybe my granny will have an explanation,' she replied, although she was already thinking that she would be lucky to get the full story out of Sarah.

After lunch they had walked to the end of King's Parade, then down the narrow streets behind the Round Church to the late Samuel's house, which overlooked Jesus Green. His friend had had a set of keys and let them both in. It had been a strange experience, entering the home of a deceased man she did not know, peering into his life like a voyeur. The photographs of him there showed a handsome man with a kind, intelligent face and a sense of style in his dress, and Olivia felt a deep stab of regret that she had never had a chance to get to know him. She had known instinctively that she would have liked him.

From what his friend had said, he was a popular, respected figure in the university and was known particularly for his kindness and his wit. It seemed that Samuel, like her grandmother, had led a very ordinary life – except that, for some reason in the distant past, he had changed his name from Grey to Orr. That was the only clue that he had something to hide.

As she had wandered round the living room, Olivia had picked up a photograph of Samuel standing on a riverbank with a fishing rod in his hand. She had been studying it when his friend remarked,

'Oh yes, that was taken near Enniskillen. He went back most years to fish. I think he used to call on your grandmother whenever he got the chance.'

Olivia turned to look at him, her mouth wide open.

'What? Did you say he went back to Ireland regularly and met my grandmother? Are you sure? Could there be some mistake?'

'I am absolutely sure. We even had a few trips back together, when I also visited family. He loved Ireland and fishing, so it was the perfect holiday for him. He did talk a little about your grandmother – he said that, although she was his stepmother, she was more like a sister to him.'

'Well, I can't believe it. She never mentioned this to us. Never. We only became aware of his existence when he died, and Grandmother was made the executor of his will. Why on earth would she hide something like this?'

There had been nothing more to be gleaned. Samuel's friend had told her everything he was aware of. Now that Samuel and her grandmother were both dead, the world they had known was gone forever. Yet the incident at the funeral pointed to some cause of deep, dark hatred buried in the stories of their lives.

Instinct told her that there was something very strange at the heart of the matter, something involving Sarah and Samuel, and her step-uncle's will. Now that Olivia thought about it, of all the half-explained events in Sarah's life, the facts surrounding Samuel were the most puzzling.

When she had returned from Cambridge that summer, Olivia had challenged her grandmother one more time, hoping that the new information about Samuel – and particularly his trips to Ireland and his visits to her – would result in a full explanation. Sarah had fixed her with a long stare and said,

'It will all be explained in time. I will write it down and you will have your answers, but don't ask me any more about it.'

Once Sarah's funeral was over, Olivia had asked her parents if she could stay a few days in her grandmother's house and go through her papers. As neither of them felt ready to undertake the task, they had agreed. Olivia had less than a week before she returned to America, so she needed to use her time effectively. Now that she was alone in her grandmother's house she had the time and space to search for information.

She opened the door to her grandmother's study and stepped inside. She breathed deeply to calm herself, finding the experience strange after all these years. The memory of one morning, when she was only seven or eight, came flooding back...

She had found the Colonel's matches in the garden and thought she would light a fire, so she went into the study to look for some old newspapers. She discovered the tin wastepaper bin full of discarded scraps and, to the young Olivia, it only seemed natural to strike a few matches and set fire to the paper.

Sarah walked in as the flames were licking up the metal sides and black smoke was billowing through the study. She went for her, screaming at her to get out and leave her things alone, while she lifted the bin and dumped it in the garden. It was the only time her grandmother had ever lost her temper with her and she had never forgotten it. Olivia had been banned from the study and, even when she was grown-up, had never gone into the room again.

Now she steeled herself to enter. She needed to look for anything that could throw light on Sarah's past. For the first time in her life, Olivia had begun to realise that the person she knew as her grandmother was just one small part of the real Sarah. She could think of no reason for Michael O'Connell's act of spite, yet somewhere in the labyrinth of Sarah's life there had to be an explanation for it.

Olivia did not really have to search for what she was looking for. As she opened the bottom drawer of Sarah's desk, she saw a red leather notebook with an envelope pinned to it and her name clearly written in Sarah's copperplate handwriting. Olivia knew her grandmother was a meticulous record-keeper – household accounts, wages paid, money given to the church, plants bought, where they were planted and how they thrived. All the minutiae of her daily life were recorded over the years. Olivia had thought that it would have been like piecing a jigsaw together and was prepared for a long, painstaking task, but she should have known that her grandmother had made some kind of record.

'Clever old Granny,' she thought to herself, 'always one jump ahead.' Olivia opened the envelope and pulled out the note.

Lindara

September 1980

My dearest Olivia,

This is for you. It will, I hope, answer many of the questions you have pestered me with over the years. You, with that quick, clever mind of yours, were never satisfied with my explanations, but I'd made a pact that none of this would be revealed while Samuel and I were still alive, and I have kept my word. There were many times when I wanted to tell you the story so that you would understand what happened back then, and how it affected Samuel and me for the rest of our lives, but it is only now, with Samuel dead, that I feel able to write it down. I have told the truth as I know it, even when I'm not proud of what I have done, but I will let the story speak for itself.

With love always,

Granny

Olivia did a quick calculation. The letter was now six years old, so her grandmother had written it, and probably the contents of the notebook, sometime after Samuel's death in 1978.

Olivia had no inkling of the history between the O'Connells and her grandmother, but it seemed certain that the notebook would provide an explanation.

CHAPTER 3

THE VISITORS

JIM, 1930

'Come on, you boys. Mother says you are to come now.'

Sally's voice echoed and bounced across the pale morning water of Ballymacarn Lough. She waited. There was silence. Only the sound of the lonely curlew's call across the stillness. She looked. In the distance she could see the rounded purple peaks of the Mourne Mountains. She knew they were out there, but the little buggers weren't answering.

'You have to come this minute or there will be trouble.' She waited. The sun sparkled on the water and the bell on Ballymacarn Church struck the hour. If they didn't come soon, she would be in trouble. Mother had given her strict instructions to have Jim clean, ready and dressed by ten o'clock sharp.

'Jim … Tom. Can you hear me?'

Still nothing. God, maybe they had taken off up to the Cromies' to get out of the road. She wouldn't put it past them, but, if they had gone, she would really be in for it. It was her job to get Jim sorted and organised, and the visitors were due in half an hour. She scanned the loughside but there was no sign of them. She waited, looking down across the field to the water's edge, where the bulrushes rose in stiff spiky bushes. Then she saw the slightest movement and she knew they were there. Looking for moorhens' nests and trying to get an egg or two, she wouldn't mind betting.

'I see you. Come on now. You have to get cleaned up and ready.'

There was a slight twitch at the edge of the rushes and then she saw a blonde head bobbing up. The head turned and registered her presence, then went down again into the undergrowth.

'That's it. Just come on now, both of you.' She watched as the two heads appeared above the level of the reeds, one as blonde as the Viking marauders he was descended from and one dark and glossy. Slowly they walked up the field, both intent on the contents of Jim's hand.

'So, what have you got there?' Two pairs of bright eyes lifted to hers.

'Look at this, Sally. We found a moorhen's nest and got an egg each. We left some there so they'll be able to hatch all right.'

Sally looked at the open hand extended to her. Jim's fingers were already grubby, but that was nothing unusual, and in the palm of his hand lay a pair of grey, mottled eggs. A moorhen's egg was a real treasure, as they built their nests on the edge of the water in the middle of the rushes and they were generally impossible to reach from the shore. The loughside was far too marshy, so if you tried to get to the nest the boggy land gave way on you. The boys had been trying to raid the moorhen's nest for two weeks with no success.

'How did you manage it, Jim?'

He looked at her with eyes that melted her heart but said nothing. Then she glanced down at his feet.

'Where are your good shoes?' He kept his eyes on the eggs in his hand and said nothing. 'I said, where are your shoes? Have you left them at the loughside?' Once again there was silence and not a word or a glance was exchanged between the two boys, but she knew they were covering something up.

'Right, then. You can go back down there this minute and get them. I've strict instructions to get you shipshape for the visitors, so just go down there and get those shoes.'

The two of them shuffled around uneasily. Then Jim turned, and with a look of defiance said,

'Who are they anyway, these visitors who are so important?'

'Don't know myself, really. A lady and a man are coming to see Mother about something, and we are all to be clean and tidy, especially you, Jim. And look at the cut of you.'

They both surveyed him in silence. He looked a state. He had no shoes and his socks were covered in thick mud up to the calf. His best grey flannel trousers were creased and wrinkled. His grey pullover looked fine enough but the tie that should have been neatly under his shirt collar was hanging loose, the knot pulled untidily to one side. Sally stepped forward and straightened it, pushing it tight up to his neck.

'Oh, leave off, will you, Sally? That's really uncomfortable.'

'You leave it now. It looks good.'

'God, I hate visitors. I don't see why I should wear a tie anyhow.'

'Stop swearing. You're not to swear.'

He looked at her and turned back to the contents of his grubby hand.

'They're brilliant, Jim. Just brilliant,' said Tom. He was altogether the easier of the two, calm and compliant by nature, in contrast to Jim's contrary, headstrong nature.

'Stop changing the subject. Where are your shoes?' asked Sally.

'I lost them in the mud.'

'You did what?'

'Oh, for goodness' sake, stop shouting, Sally. It's not the end of the world.'

'Shoes cost money, Jim, and it is money we don't have, as you rightly know.'

'Oh, don't worry, Sally. I'll do some extra milking to pay for a new pair. Just leave me alone.'

'I'll do nothing of the sort. Come this minute and get ready or I'll tell Mother about the shoes.'

They turned and walked up the field together, the two boys both intent on the eggs. They climbed the gate and crossed the lane to the house.

'Come around this way and don't let Mother see you,' Sally said. They tiptoed round the side of the house and Sally met them at the barn with a big bowl of water and a cloth. 'Here you are. Get those socks off and get your legs washed right away.'

The socks were coated in mud, but they would wash. It was the missing shoes that would cause the trouble.

'Here, wash your hands now and I will get you some other shoes. I suppose you will have to wear your gutties, for they're all you've got.'

'Aw, they'll be all right. The visitors won't be looking at my feet. Now, just quit worrying.'

Sally's thin frame disappeared indoors. The boys waited in the old barn sitting on a bale of hay. Tom was eleven, a year older than Jim. They were as close as blood brothers, even though Jim had been fostered by the family when he was a tiny baby. The years went by and he stayed with the family, aware that he was not truly one of them, but nobody bothered about that small fact.

'I'll just put the eggs away somewhere safe,' said Jim. He reached up to a shelf and pulled down an old battered wooden box. It was where he kept all his treasures. He opened the lid and pulled some hay from the bale. Then he put it into the box and laid the eggs carefully down on it. He replaced the lid and set the box back up on the shelf. 'There. They should be safe now and we'll come back to look at them when the visitors have gone.'

'That's them now,' said Tom, and they both listened to the sound of a car turning into the lane.

'Jim, come here this minute and get your clean socks and gutties on. The visitors are here.'

Sally set down the items. She had cleaned the gutties as best she could in the short time she had, but they still weren't great. The rubber around the soles and the toecaps had come up all right but the canvas part, which was meant to be white, was still a mucky brown.

'I just hope the visitors don't pay too much attention to your feet.'

'Stop worrying, Sally.'

'Let's go round and see the car,' said Tom.

They went to the front of the house and saw that a black shiny motor car was parked on the flat grass across from the house.

'Wow, that's a beauty.'

'They must be rich, these visitors. I wonder why they are visiting us.'

'They're staying at the Spa Hotel,' Tom informed him.

'Then they really must have money.'

The two boys ranged round the car, inspecting every bit of it.

'I want to see the engine,' Jim said. 'I wonder if they would let me if I asked.'

'I'm sure they would,' replied Tom. 'No reason why not.'

They stood and looked at the machine with admiration.

'It's a lot better than Cromie's old banger,' said Tom.

'Ach, sure, there's no comparison,' Jim agreed.

'Come here, boys,' Ellen's voice called from the garden. They looked at each other with a grin and headed across the lane. The visitors were of interest now that they had such a fine black shiny car.

Ellen had seats laid out in the garden and the two visitors, a man and a woman, sat drinking tea out of the best china cups. They were both well dressed. The man was tall with dark hair and smiley brown eyes, and he looked very friendly. The woman sat slightly apart from him on the other side of the table. She was tall, slim and sat very erect on the beechwood chair. There was a cold look in her steely grey eyes, and something in the way she sat, and the way she looked at them, told the boys she would rather not be there.

Jim glanced at his mother and saw the slightest of frowns cross her face when her eyes lit on his gutties. Nothing was said. It didn't need to be.

'Here are the boys now. Tom and Jim, I want you to say hello to Mr and Mrs Brown.'

They both looked over and said hello, still unclear about who the visitors were.

'Are you related to us, then, if you're called Brown?' Jim asked. He had never heard of any rich relatives.

'I don't suppose you've any idea who this lady and gentleman are, do you?' asked Ellen. Both boys stared at her, while the visitors said nothing. Their minds were turning over. Slow recognition was starting to form.

Jim looked hard at both strangers, taking in their features. He had vague memories of a man and a woman like these two visiting before, many years ago. He stared again at them, and the suspicion in his mind slowly began to take shape. He often used to wonder if this day would ever come but now, just a few months short of his eleventh birthday, he knew that the day he used to dream about was finally here. Now that his dream had come true, he wasn't sure he wanted it after all.

'I have a surprise for you, Jim,' said Ellen. 'This is your mother and father.'

There was silence as they all stared at each other.

'But you're my mother. I haven't got any mother but you,' said Jim, who was the first to recover from the shock.

'Och, now, Jim, sure you always knew you were fostered with us. We never made any secret of the fact. You always knew that. You knew your father and mother would come for you one day. It just took a long time for that day to come and now they're here.'

Jim stared at Ellen without speaking and then moved his eyes to the strangers.

'But why have you come now? It's been years, and I don't want to go and live with you. I want to stay here with Mother, Sally and Tom and all my family and friends.'

The man rose and went around the table to stand in front of Jim, then got down on his hunkers so that he could look him in the eye.

'Now, Jim, we know that Ellen has looked after you all these years, but it was only because your mother and I couldn't look after you ourselves. It is a bit complicated to explain, but we are going to make up for it now. You see, we got a letter and it made us realise that you really need some good schooling, so we are planning to send you to one of the best. You are very bright, and you deserve a good education.'

'Hang on a minute. What is all this about a good school? The Spa school is brilliant. I'm always top of the class, especially in sums, and what's this about a letter? What letter?'

Ellen and Sally exchanged glances, and Jim could see that they were both uncomfortable. Ellen pulled a sheet from her pocket and held it out to him.

'Here's the letter. You had better read it.'

The Spa
Ballynahinch

Dear Mr Brown,

I hope you will not take me writing to you as an impertinence, but I do so in a friendly spirit. I have watched your son Jim with interest, and I am greatly pleased with the way he has turned out. He is a clever boy who deserves more than the basic education of a village school. His family look after him well and have given him a clean outlook on life, but they cannot give him the opportunity for higher learning that he is capable of.

I am only an onlooker and may be wrong, but were I blessed with children I would like to see them succeed and carry on my name after me. I will not sign this in case it calls up any bad feeling, but I am certain your boy would be happy in his own home with the opportunities you could offer him. Will you not give him a chance?

A friend of your son

The letter was carefully constructed and typed on good paper. Jim knew immediately who the author was. It could only be Miss Henderson. She was always on at him to study and do his best, and he was her class favourite. What was she doing sticking her nose in? She meant well, but he had no intention of going anywhere with two strangers.

Mr Brown knew what he was thinking and interrupted his thoughts.

'Jim, Tom, why don't we go and have a look at the car? I am sure you would like that.'

'Not half,' they answered together, their eyes shining.

'Well, come on, then, and take a look.'

He rose and led the way out to the lane where the car was parked. The boys crawled all over it examining every aspect of it in detail.

'Can I see the engine, please?' Jim asked politely.

'Of course you can. Come around here. This is where the bonnet catches are, and you have to undo them like this to open the bonnet.'

The boys watched as he flipped the catches and lifted the shiny black metal. They both stared into the engine compartment.

'Look at this, Tom.' Jim's eyes danced with pleasure. 'This has been so well looked after. The engine's as clean as anything.'

'I have a man who looks after the car for me and he does a grand job of it. Ned is his name.'

'That's what I want to do when I grow up. I am going to be the best mechanic and engineer in the whole of Ireland,' said Jim.

'He will too,' said Tom. 'He can fix anything that goes wrong with the Cromies' car, even though he's only ten. He helps them with the tractor too.'

'Is that right?' Mr Brown ruffled his hair. 'And what are you going to do when you grow up?'

'Oh, I am going to work on the farm. I love the farm,' replied Tom.

They chatted and chuckled and gave the car a full going-over, even taking turns to get behind the wheel and steer.

'He's nice, this Mr Brown,' thought Jim. He knew a lot about the car and the speed it could do, all the details about the engine, and he was very easy to be with. He seemed very kind, but it was hard to think of him as his father. Willie Brown was his dad and he was the only dad he had ever known, but he was so different to the man who stood before Jim now.

He knew he didn't belong to the family who had fostered him. He'd always known he had come to the family as a three-day-old baby. But the years had gone by and he had rarely thought about his real parents or why they had fostered him. It seemed they had virtually forgotten him all these years. He'd got on with growing up and doing all the usual things boys do, and now he was presented with these two strangers who claimed to be his parents, all because Miss Henderson had decided to write them a letter.

'Come and get your tea now, Mr Brown, before it gets cold,' Ellen called from the garden.

Mr Brown winked at them and put a hand on each boy's

shoulder to guide them into the garden.

'Better get in there before we get into trouble.' Ellen poured fresh tea from a big brown teapot. She'd managed china cups, but she had never got to acquire the china teapot to match them. The boys stood to one side, not sure what to do with themselves. They both took sidelong looks at the lady, but she seemed distant and unapproachable, not at all like Mr Brown. Up to the present she had shown little interest in her son, Jim. She just sat there, ramrod straight, sipping her tea as if it was poison and not speaking to anyone.

'So, you plan to come back for Jim in two days, then?' Ellen asked.

'Yes, we will leave on Friday. I take it you can have him ready by then.'

Jim watched as big tears rolled down Ellen's cheeks and her shoulders quivered. She was trying to keep up a front but not succeeding, and then Sally started a long, low, keening sob.

'Well, I am not going anywhere with you,' Jim exclaimed. 'I'm staying here where I belong, so mind that.'

With that, he and Tom took to their heels and ran out of the gate, across the lane and down the field, back to the safety of the loughside, where nobody could find them.

Chapter 4

DEPARTURES

Jim, 1930

After much discussion and shouting on Jim's part, it was agreed that Tom would go with him on the journey and stay until the last week of the school holidays to help Jim settle in. They huddled in the back of the car, watching the countryside go by. The car seats were made of rich black leather and they had never enjoyed such luxury in their short lives, but it did not make up for the sadness Jim felt at leaving the Spa. The departure had been chaotic. The Cromies from next door said their goodbyes first, with no great stress or emotion. Then the Browns came out in force. There was Robbie, Nelly, Susan, Jane, Mima, Harry and Sally, as well as Willie and Ellen. Even with all the noise and the ballyhoo of the family calling their farewells and demanding letters and postcards, Jim could clearly hear Ellen's loud sobs above the clamour. She kept murmuring,

'It's all for the best. It's all for the best. You'll get your schooling now.' But then, her large chest heaving, she would break down again.

They only got away in the end by Father agreeing that Jim and Tom would come back in time for the Ballynahinch Show. Father made a promise to the Browns, and said he would make sure Ned drove them both.

Jim became more subdued as they passed through the string of small towns on the way to his new home. The green patchwork fields of Ulster sped by outside the car window. He had never been this far from home before, and with the miles the landscape changed from the hilly drumlins of County Down to the rolling orchard lands of County Armagh.

Then the car slowed and turned into a narrow lane bordered on both sides by hawthorn hedges covered in white may blossom. On the hill ahead he could see a grand stone house. It was a large, classic Irish country house of Georgian design, built in grey stone with symmetrical white windows and a delicately patterned fanlight over the front door.

'I think this must be it,' he whispered to Tom.

The car slid to a halt at the front door and Mr Brown turned to him and smiled.

'This is your new home. Jim and Tom, you are both very welcome.'

They jumped from the car and surveyed the house and its surroundings. To a boy of ten who had never been further than twenty miles from home, it was a new world. The grandeur of the place was the stuff of dreams, and it was difficult to take in that this was to be his new home. The sadness and the apprehension he had felt at leaving his adopted home and family were dispersed by the excitement of this new world.

'Come and I will show you around the place,' Mr Brown called from the steps. They followed him in for the grand tour of Carrick House, going from room to room in quiet awe.

'Did you ever see the like of it?' Jim whispered to Tom as they were shown around.

'They have the best of everything here. It is a world and a half away from our house and the Cromies,' Tom whispered back.

'Even electric lights in every room.'

'And inside bathrooms.'

They were almost speechless with the grandeur of the place.

'Imagine what the boys at the Spa would say if they could see us now. Do you know, Tom, we will never forget coming here till the day we die.'

'We'll go and see the yard now, if you like,' Mr Brown said. 'I suppose you would like to see the garage.'

They went into the yard, and at one end they could see the garage with the door flung open and a second car parked inside.

'Here's Ned,' Mr Brown said, as he brought the boys into the garage. 'Ned, these are the boys, Jim and Tom, and I think you will be seeing a lot of the two of them in the next while, especially Jim, as he is really keen on cars.'

'Oh, that'll be fine with me, sir,' Ned replied. 'I'm only too happy to teach you anything you want to know about cars and engines. They are my pride and joy, aren't they, sir?'

Jim's eyes lit on the end wall of the garage. Ranged along it was a huge array of tools, and the whole wall had been organised so that all the implements hung in sets, going from small to large. There were hammers of all shapes and sizes hooked onto nails, which had been driven into the wall at just the right distance to hold them. Then screwdrivers, saws and spanners. To the right there was a cabinet with rows and rows of drawers, each with its contents listed. All the sizes and types of nails, screws, washers and nuts were there and everything was clean, tidy and organised.

'Did you ever see the like of it, Tom?' Jim said, as he gazed spellbound at the display of tools before him.

'Boy, this is brilliant,' said Tom.

Ned called them from the other side of the garage.

'Come and see the mistress's car. It's a beauty.'

They looked at each other and both pulled a face. So, the lady could drive, could she? Maybe she was more interesting than they imagined. To date she had been cold and formal with them, but if she could drive a car maybe she was due more attention. They looked the vehicle over, and it was every bit as impressive as the one they had come in from the Spa. There was such a lot to see and take in – more than was possible all at once.

'Better get yourself over to the house and get cleaned up for tea,' Mr Brown called from the back of the garage, where he was talking to Ned. 'You boys go on and I will be over in a minute.'

They crossed the yard and Tom slowed to look at Jim.

'Well, what do you think?'

'Better than I thought. I might as well give it a try for a while,' and they chuckled together as they crossed the yard to the house.

***

Fair View
Spa
Ballynahinch

14 June 1930

Dear Jim,

We were greatly disappointed we did not have a letter from you and were wondering if you are not well. It will soon work round to the show. The cat has kittled and has two lovely wee kittens: one white, one grey and white. Mother does not feel very well when you do not write. Mother said when she sent you stamps she wondered why you didn't write.

Love to Jim from Sally

***

Fair View
Spa
Ballynahinch

16 June 1930

Dear Jim,

We wondered why you never wrote or did you never get the six stamps? Jim, write and let us know how you are getting on. Mother is thinking of you late and early, so I think that is all for present.

Love to Jim from Sally

***

Fair View
Spa
Ballynahinch

20 June 1930

Dear Jim,

I hope you are keeping well. Mother was delighted to get your letter yesterday morning to help lift her heart. Write back and let us know how you are getting on. You need not be expecting them on Sunday but hope to see you at Ballynahinch Show. All the boys from school are sending you postcards and are you ever getting any of them? I am sending you a stamped envelope. Do not forget to write to Mother. It will help to lift her heart.

Love to Jim from Sally

***

Fair View
Spa
Ballynahinch

30 June 1930

Dear Jim,

We were greatly disappointed to hear you will not be getting to Ballynahinch Show. Mother got second prize for her soda bread. We are always getting letters and they help to lift Mother's heart. Everybody is asking about you. Jack got three firsts and two seconds, and one of the firsts was for the big bull. Mrs McCoubrey got a first in the wild flowers and a highly recommended for a dog. Robbie's wife and I were at the show and saw the horse jumping. Jimmy Hamey was on the horse jumping. Sam Heanan got second for his cow. I think that is all for the present.

Love to Jim from Sally

***

Ned had been called away to a family funeral, so he hadn't been able to drive Jim and Tom back for the Ballynahinch Show as planned. There were great ructions, and the boys were so upset.

They were determined to get back for as much of the holidays as they could, and it was finally agreed that they would go back to the Spa for the last part of the summer.

Ned drove them there, and everyone at the Spa turned out to welcome them. In no time they had slotted back into their old routines. Jim loved being with his old friends and having the freedom to roam the countryside that he knew so well. A week turned into two, then three. Jim became adamant that he wasn't ready to go back to Carrick House until the holidays were over, but he seemed to accept the fact that he would eventually be leaving for the new school in Armagh.

***

Fair View
Spa
Ballynahinch

24 July 1930

Dear Father,

I hope you are well. Just a few lines to let you know I am staying here another week. Tom is coming back with me for a few weeks until I settle into school.

Yours truly,
Jim

***

In the middle of August, Ned was sent to collect the boys and bring them back to Carrick House. Tom went with Jim to keep him company, and it was agreed he would stay for a week or two. The leaving was much calmer this time, and only Ellen and Sally saw them off. Jim seemed to feel easier now that he knew he could come and go between the two houses and the move didn't seem quite so permanent. He would go to school in Armagh but come back to the Spa for holidays.

On an afternoon in September the boys were sitting on the bank of the small river, their nets stretched out into the still, dark pool just beyond the weeds.

'I hate this house and I hate the school,' Jim suddenly exploded. 'I am not going to put up with it any longer. I'm going back to the Spa.'

Tom hesitated. He was more cautious by nature than Jim and inclined to weigh things up much more carefully.

'But they won't let you.'

'I don't need to be let. I'm going and that's that.'

There was silence for a minute.

'Well, I don't like it here either but at least I am going home at the end of next week. I miss Sally and Mother and all my friends, and I just want to be back up at the farm helping Mr Cromie with the cows and the hens. Your father is OK, and I really like Ned, but I don't like your mother much, do you?'

'Oh, there's no pleasing her no matter what,' Jim replied tartly.

'What are you going to do?'

'I've planned it all out already. We'll write to Sally and Jane and get them to borrow the Cromies' car and drive it here to take us home.'

'Do you think they'll do it?'

'Aye, they'll do it, all right. Jane is game for anything and they will all be glad to see me back.'

They both dabbled their nets half-heartedly in the water, knowing they had very little chance of catching anything, but were happy just to be by the river in the September sunshine.

'We should never have come back from the Spa at the end of the summer holidays. You should just have stayed there,' said Tom.

'Well, it's easy to say that now, but I didn't know how bad school was going to be. They said it was a great place, with sports and everything, so how was I to know what it was really like?'

'Well, they were wrong. You hate that school and you know it will never be as good as the Spa. None of the masters could be as good as Mr McConkey. I know I'd rather have my school any day than that posh place.'

'Not so much homework at the Spa either,' said Jim. He pondered for a minute and then said, 'Right, I am going back, and that's agreed.'

Tom grinned with delight at the thought of Jim coming back with him.

'Get your pen and paper, and get writing.'

At school, Jim couldn't settle to work at all. He was too excited. The plan was all set, and now he just had to wait. He gazed at his sums but for once they just wouldn't go in. Normally mathematics was no trouble to him. Any kind of problems he could do them 100 per cent right, and in half the time it took the rest of the class.

'You, Brown. Stop staring out of the window and get on with your work,' the teacher bellowed at him.

Jim focused on the page and did the first few questions.

'Will they be able to find the way all right?' he wondered. The original plan had been to borrow the Cromies' car, but Mrs Cromie got wind of it and wouldn't hear of them coming to take Jim back. She'd put the mockers on it the first time, but now Jane and Sally had hatched some scheme or other for borrowing the car with Mrs Cromie none the wiser. All Jim could think was,

'What if she finds out about it and puts a stop to it again?'

'Brown, what's got into you today?' the teacher asked. 'Stop staring out of the window like a zombie. If you don't get your work done, you'll get detention and you can do it then.'

Well, detention was the last thing he needed. Then if they did come, there would be only Tom there to meet them and he wouldn't know what had happened. The fright of it made him concentrate, and in no time the sums were done.

'There you are, sir. All done.'

'I hope they are done as well as usual, Brown.'

'Yes, sir,' Jim replied. Five minutes more and school would be out. Ned usually collected him in his father's car. He seemed to be looked after mostly by either Ned or Kate when Father was at work, but Father was home every evening and was always interested in how Jim was and how he was getting on at school.

Mother, as he now had to call her, was away on business a lot, but that in itself was a relief. When she was at home there was no pleasing her. She would say things like,

'Do this, do that, mind your manners, eat like this, talk like that.' Then she would come out with her constant refrain,

'Polite people do it like this, or in good company people always do it that way.' Jim felt like saying more than once,

'Who gives a bugger?' But then that would only stir up

trouble, and she was bad enough as it was. So far, he had managed to hold his tongue, but he knew it couldn't last. One day he would tell her what she could do with her polite manners.

The bell rang for the end of school. They were out in a bundle of bags and hats and blazers into the bright sunlight of a September afternoon. The car was at the bottom of the school drive with Ned at the wheel waiting to take him home.

Ned had grown fond of Jim, for in the short time that he had been at Carrick he and Tom had brought life into the house. He was forever up at the garage asking about the cars and how things worked, and trying his hand at some of the easier tasks on the engines. Both the boys were interested but Jim was the one with the real flair for 'mechanic-ing', as Ned liked to call it. He was a natural.

Tom's gifts lay with the animals about the place. Already Shot and Sooner, the red setters, followed him about like a shadow. The boys had roared with laughter when Ned explained to them that the dogs got their names because, when you called them, one came like a shot and the other came sooner or later.

'There you are,' Ned said as he pulled into the yard. Jim could see Tom waiting for him by the doors of the garage. 'Don't be long getting changed and I'll show you how to swap a gasket.'

'Poor auld fellow hasn't got a clue of our intentions, has he?' Jim said as they walked into the house.

'He'll miss you. He likes having you around and showing you how to work on the cars,' said Tom.

'We'll miss him too, but it doesn't make up for the rest of it.'

'Oh, I know. You're right there.'

Jim changed quickly out of his school uniform and went into the kitchen for a scone and some milk. Kate was pottering around as usual, seeing to his needs.

'We're off out now, Kate. See you at supper time.'

They grinned at each other as they walked off down the drive.

'See you at supper time,' indeed. It would be a fair few suppers before Kate would see them again, if everything went to plan. Provided the car made it. Provided they didn't have an accident.

They walked as fast as their legs would carry them down the road. The rendezvous point was the junction of the Armagh and Portadown roads, where there was a big chestnut tree. They could see the tree in the distance but there was no sign of the car.

Jim's heart sank. Oh, what if they didn't come? What if Mrs Cromie had found out again and put the mockers on it? Maybe it was all a hoax and Sally and Jane had no intention of taking them away from this mother and father, who claimed to be his but were not a real mother and father like Ellen and Willy.

They both heard the engine at the same time and looked at each other for confirmation.

'Can you hear it?'

'Yeah, sure can.'

They listened, and the sound became more defined and clearer. It was a car engine, and they both knew so well the sound of the Cromies' old banger.

'We should hide in the ditch until we're sure it is them,' Tom suggested.

'You're right.' They huddled down behind the bank at the

side of the road and watched the junction by the big tree. A black car came into view and slowed, then stopped. Jim made to move but Tom held him back.

'Just a wee minute. Let's make sure it's them.'

'Look,' Jim exclaimed, 'it's them, all right. It's the Austin and it's the right number plate: BZ 387.'

The car stood still, and there was no movement for a moment. They watched but didn't budge, and no one got out. It just sat at the junction, immobile. Then the driver's door opened, and they saw the rotund figure of Jane emerge. They were out of the ditch and running along the road before Sally had time to get out of the passenger's side.

'We're here, we're here,' they roared.

The two sisters grabbed the boys and hugged them.

'Och, sure, it seems weeks since we saw you last,' said Sally. 'Are you ready, then?'

'Too true,' they roared together.

'Off to the Spa, then. Get in quick before anybody sees you and tells your father.'

They clambered into the car, the doors banged closed, and then the car circled the big chestnut and drove quickly back the way it had come.

Back to the Spa.

Chapter 5

THE PIG TEA PARTY

Sarah, 1910

I know exactly when the track of my life went off course and I can recall, precisely, every detail of that day. I remember it was a cool day in June, that I was wearing my new blue dress, and that everyone else remembered it for the disruption of the tea party at Lindara House.

I can still see the tables laid out for the party on the lawns in front of the house, their pure white linen tablecloths touching the grass. The tables were piled high with sandwiches, scones, homemade cakes and buns, as they were every year. The villagers would arrive dressed in their best and take part in the games, the competitions and the old-fashioned country pursuits. There was never any strong drink, for that would only lead to rowdy behaviour, but there was always fresh lemonade, milk or ginger beer available during the afternoon until tea was served.

Before that day my life was all planned out in my mind. I had loved Hugh with a passion since the day I first saw him, and I knew I would marry him, live in Lindara House, raise our children and organise our lives between the estate in Ireland and the house in London when he eventually succeeded to the title. Until then, I imagined us at the pinnacle of local society.

Hugh had been a part of my life for as long as I could remember. When Father went to advise Lord Clanhugh, Hannah and

I used to go with him and we would roam the grounds together with Hugh, skim stones on the lake, or play hide-and-seek in the attics. Later, when we were older, there were races on the top field on the ponies Mistral and Scirocco.

Hannah, of course, was part of the game but it was Hugh and I who were the daredevils, the partners in hellraising and adventure. Poor Hannah, who was two years older than me and much more sensible, would try to tame us and make us more thoughtful and responsible, but we only laughed at her and egged each other on to greater mischief. Hannah was always the one left behind, ever on the edge of the world that belonged to Hugh and me. He was my first love, my first kiss, my sweetheart.

Our closeness lasted throughout his years at school and university in England. He came home for holidays and I knew to the minute when he would arrive. I used the servants and their gossip to find out when he was due, and I was always there at the window of the drawing room when he went past. Then, in no time, we would pick up where we left off, the months of separation would fall away, and we would be soulmates again. There was no one else who mattered in my world except Hugh – parents, family, servants and friends were around me, but not central to me in the way he was. Even Hannah was never the core of my life the way Hugh was.

The Lindara tea party was held every summer, and had been started by Hugh's mother in an attempt to encourage social harmony in our small village. Well meant though it was, it was naive to expect that the social divide and long-held hatred could be wiped out in one afternoon.

I remember that year in particular because Hugh was supposed to be home the day prior to the party, but there was a storm the night before that delayed the ship crossing from England. The message that got through wasn't clear, and even the servants' grapevine hadn't managed to establish when he was due. All we knew was that he was on his way, and he would be home as soon as possible. Then he would be there for the whole summer, and we could ride and walk and talk as long as we wanted to.

The day of the party was overcast and blustery, not unusual for a June day in Ulster. Theodore Grey's car pulled up at the house at 2 p.m. to collect us. His tall figure stepped out of the car and made a slight bow.

'Let me help you,' he said to Hannah, as he took her by the elbow and steered her into the car. I remember Hannah's sweet, simpering smile, how she cast down her eyes and giggled. It was a nervous giggle caused by shyness and embarrassment at the attention he was giving her. Mr Grey was at that time a widower of sixty, and his stiff, old-fashioned mannerisms made us both less at ease than we would have been with boys of our own age.

His son, Samuel, sat quietly in the back of the car, too shy to speak to Hannah and me. He was home from boarding school for the summer, and though I'd seen him in church and around the village he was only a youngster, so I'd never looked closely at him before. As I climbed into the car, I looked at him properly for the first time, and I remember thinking that with his blonde hair, blue eyes and clear skin he was the most beautiful boy I'd ever seen.

I was not one bit pleased with the attention Theo was paying

Hannah, but the most surprising thing was that my parents did not seem to agree with me. I had suggested to Mother only the month before that Theo seemed to be courting Hannah, but she showed little concern. Perhaps it was something to do with the fact that he owned half of Lindara, and the part he owned was the moneymaking part.

Theo owned the mill that provided most of the employment in the village and gave prosperity to the whole area. He also owned a lot of the property – the pub, the hotel, the shop and most of the houses, which were rented out to his millworkers. The other half was owned by the Clanhughs, so between them you could say that the two families owned most of West Armagh.

Although he was rich, to me he was no kind of a husband for Hannah. I thought she should have her heart set on someone nearer her own age. A young blade, or at the very least a son of one of the wealthy farming families. There were plenty of takers for a girl like Hannah, yet she seemed to accept the attentions of Theo quite happily. At times she even seemed to encourage him.

The car swept through the gates of Lindara estate and I looked at Theo with a wince of distaste. He was tall and lanky, with a lean face and grey hair. His moustache was carefully barbered and trimmed, and he was decked out in the finest of clothes. His white shirt with its high wing collar, dark tie, grey suit and moleskin waistcoat came from the best tailors in Armagh, but, for all his polish and wealth, he was an old man. There was no getting away from that.

As his long, pale hands gripped the steering wheel, I imagined them fondling Hannah, and the thought of it made me shiver. The image of them together was utterly strange to me – so different from Hugh and me, who were so right for each other.

The party was just getting under way when we arrived, and Billy O'Connell stepped over to the car as it drew up to the steps of Lindara House.

'Lovely dress, Miss Sarah,' he said, leaning forward to stroke the blue satin.

'Get your hands off this minute, Billy. You'll ruin it and then you'll be in trouble,' I said.

'Lovely dress,' he persisted. I swiped his hands off the dress before he could dirty it. Why, oh why, did I have to be the centre of attraction for halfwits? Billy was always drawn to me when our paths crossed. He would sidle up to me out of the blue and stare at me in adoration with dumb cows' eyes.

'Just go away and leave me alone now. Do you hear?' I spoke harshly to him, for there was no point in being soft with Billy or he wouldn't understand. He would just have seen it as encouragement and then he would have followed me around all day.

'Billy, here's a penny for the games. Off you go and enjoy yourself like a good boy,' Hannah said, giving him a gentle pat on the head. She was always able to be kind to Billy even when all I ever felt was irritation, but I was the one he followed around and I was the one who had to put up with his gawks and stares.

I scanned the whole of the garden and saw Lord and Lady Clanhugh mingling with the crowds. All the faces were familiar to me, but I couldn't see the face I was looking for. Hugh had still not arrived. There were various games under way, and every so often the crowd would break into a cheer as someone hit a coconut or knocked over all the skittles. Faces appeared before me and I smiled or passed the time of day, but it was all done out of habit for my heart was not in it. My mind was elsewhere, and I wouldn't be able to settle until I could see Hugh and stand beside him and smile into his eyes.

The day was interminable for me and though I managed to keep up some pretence at sociability, my impatience began to show as the day wore on and the car still hadn't arrived. Then I heard it – the clear and unmistakable sound of an engine.

The car swung around the corner and drove into the stable yard at the back of the house. I wandered down towards the lake because I didn't want my feelings to show. Of course Hugh wouldn't be fooled. I knew he would be anxious to see me, but there were certain rules to be observed. I couldn't run into his arms or he into mine. I would have to smile and greet him and pretend that only friendship existed between us.

Then he was on the steps of the house, framed in the doorway, taking in the scene before him. Even at a distance I could see him breathing in the cool, clear summer air scented with roses and lavender and freshly cut grass. He was home to his beloved Lindara after the exile an English education imposed on him, and he would be here all summer, released from the rigours of the study that he cared little for into the work of the estate that he loved.

I remember that I had just started to cross the lawn to greet him. His mother and father were at his side, and Lady Clanhugh was kissing his cheek while his father had a hand on his shoulder.

The scene is frozen in my mind, for it was then that a young woman appeared through the door and joined the family group. At first I did not understand that there was anything amiss. I did not immediately think it odd that a beautiful, well groomed and extremely well dressed young lady was standing by his side.

I observed but could not hear the introductions. Hugh was presenting her to his mother and father, and he had one hand solicitously around her waist.

I had not heard of any visitor, yet she was obviously a stranger to the family. Whoever she was, she cut a fine figure against the backdrop of Lindara House and she certainly had wealth and breeding behind her, that was obvious. The realisation built gradually in my mind as I watched Hugh guide her through the introductions with the small family circle.

Then he made the introductions to Mother, Father, Hannah and Theo, and my stomach knotted.

When Hannah told me, I had already guessed. That part of me which had always been in tune with Hugh from our youngest days knew without words being said. Rage erupted through me and there was a great roaring in my ears like the Blackwater rushing over the weir in full flood. My eyes focused on Hugh and his fiancée, but I saw them through a haze. I had no idea of time or place, but I kept control. Training, manners and ritual came to my rescue. I smiled, spoke, nodded, while inside I churned.

I saw my life shattered and broken because I couldn't any longer expect to become Lady Clanhugh. I would not live in Lindara House, visit London in the season or be at the top of the social life in the county. The best I could now hope for was marriage to one of the wealthier families around, but that would not give me what should have been mine, for it was only Hugh I wanted.

Now what did I have to look forward to? Marriage to one of the local lads who had no style? Life on some farm with the husband who would work on the land and sit in front of me at night smelling of cabbages and pigs? Perhaps marriage to one of the professional sons in Armagh, where I would have to compete with the social horde and beg for enough money to buy a decent wardrobe. I knew it from the friends of my parents. I could see what their lives were like and I knew what to expect. It fell a long way short of the life I had dreamt of with Hugh.

And what if Hannah married Theo? They'd been together all afternoon, and the idea that he was courting her seriously was now difficult to ignore. That would provide Hannah with wealth and status well beyond me.

I went through the formal introductions without betraying for one moment my true feelings. Hugh would not look me in the eye. He knew how I felt, and Hannah guessed, but no one else had a clue.

The tea was finally being served, and everyone gathered round the long tables at the front of the house. The villagers sat on the grass in groups, chatting happily, but I couldn't bring myself to sit with them because eating would have been an impossibility. I slipped away quietly round the back of the house towards the kitchen garden, unnoticed by anyone. I had to be on my own.

As I rounded the end of the kitchen garden the tears were rolling down my cheeks and I couldn't control my sobbing.

Then I stopped in my tracks as I saw Billy leaning over the half-door of the end stable. He heard me and looked up, his big soft, halfwit eyes brimming with tears of sympathy when he saw mine. It cut me to the quick to see pity in the eyes of the village idiot and to know it was for me. I was not to be pitied.

'Are you crying, Miss Sarah?' he asked.

'No. I am not, Billy. It is just something in my eye. What are you doing here anyway?' I asked crossly.

'Only looking at the wee pigs, Miss Sarah. Lovely wee pigs. The sow has got a big litter.'

I peered over the half-door of the stable, and there was one of the prize pigs with her litter. The home farm was over the other side of the lake but sometimes, if there was a sickly sow that needed a lot of attention, it would be brought over to the end stable to be nursed to health.

Then the idea came to me, and even in my turmoil I smiled to myself. As we turned to leave, I slipped the bar in the door and eased it slightly open. It would only be a matter of time before one of the piglets pushed against the door and found a way out.

'Off you go, Billy. Your mum is waiting for you at the front of the house. The tea is being served, and if you don't hurry you'll miss out on all the buns.'

His eyes lit up at the mention of food and he ambled off with his gawky, rolling gait, across the stable yard towards the front lawn. I made my way back through the kitchen garden, leaving by the end gate that led to the wood and then cutting through the trees onto the drive.

As I rounded the bend in the avenue, the sow and her litter came around the side of the house and made for the tables. I will never forget the chaos. Women and children ran shrieking from the big, lumbering sow, while the men tried to catch the mother and her litter of ten, which were now running everywhere. One of the tables went over with a crash, scattering cream buns and cakes over the lawn and everyone standing near. There was complete bedlam. At the top table, Lord Clanhugh was shouting at Stokes, the farm manager, while the ladies upped skirts and headed for the safety of the house. I noticed with satisfaction that the new fiancée was the first to the front door, making sure she was safe, regardless of the other, older women.

The villagers still recall it to this day. Many of the younger ones have heard the tale, and it has been embellished over the years. Poor Billy got the blame, of course, and his reputation was founded on the incident for years. If he had been in our circle, he would have dined out on it. There was no bitterness in the blame. His lack of wits excused him from any malice.

The Clanhughs were enraged about the pigs getting out and spoiling the party, although the anger only lasted a day or two, and then they saw the funny side of it. It was more a matter of pride that the pigs had spoilt the party in front of their grand English guest. They feared that the Irish gentry, which was always second class to the English, had been proved to be country oafs who had pigs at a tea party.

The pigs were back in the stable and the mess was cleared up but the sad thing, the frightening thing, was that the family could not see that the havoc caused by the pigs was only the minor matter. They did not realise that the day the Honourable Lucinda Parker came into the family and pushed me out was the day their future was set on the road to ruin. The day of the Pig Tea Party lives in the annals of village history, but the real significance of that day was lost on all of them except me. Somewhere deep inside I knew she would be the ruin of the Clanhughs.

For me, that day marked the end of my childhood, when I realised that the world would not bend to my will. I am ashamed to think how selfish I was, how unkind to poor Billy, yet that was nothing compared to what I then did to Hannah. Yet, with hindsight, I can see that a wrong-headed, purely selfish decision on my part set both Hannah and me off in a new direction which, in the end, was best for both of us.

Chapter 6

BELFAST

I was on the train to Belfast on Tuesday morning. I knew I would not be able to avoid meeting Hugh and Lucinda if I stayed in Lindara, so I arranged to visit my aunt in the city for a couple of weeks in the hope that they would be gone when I got back.

'It's great to see you,' Lizzie shouted as soon as she saw me at the station. 'And what brought you up to Belfast with so little notice?' She and Aunt Beatrice had come to pick me up and they hugged and kissed me as if they had not seen me for years. They had always been a much more affectionate family than ours.

'I'll tell you when we get home,' I said.

It was great to be back in Belfast with all the bustle and crowds. It was a big thriving city, where horse cabs filled the streets, crowds manoeuvred along the pavements and ladies in their finery met to shop in luxury stores like Robinson & Cleaver. The department store sat opposite the City Hall, a grand building with spacious grounds in the centre of Belfast. It was busy and lively after the bucolic charm of Lindara, and it helped to take my mind off Hugh. I was buzzing with excitement.

'Well, let's get you home and have some lunch,' Aunt B said.

Aunt B, my father's sister, was married to Tobias, a successful solicitor at a renowned law firm in the city. They lived in a large house on Malone Road, close to the university and the Botanic Gardens, with their children George and Lizzie.

Their family life was hugely different to ours. It was full of theatre, music, bridge, golf, tennis, dinner parties and a close involvement in local politics. Meals were always lively, with discussions ranging over many subjects, and the most interesting thing was that the females in the house were as forthcoming in their opinions as the males. What is more, they were expected to argue and express their point of view. I loved getting involved in their discussions and testing my ability to debate. It was so different to our house, where Mother and Hannah would never cross words with my father. His word was law.

After lunch we went to Lizzie's bedroom, and she immediately turned to me.

'Well, what brought you here so suddenly? I know you too well. Something is up.'

'It's Hugh. He came back to Lindara on Saturday and he brought his fiancée with him,' I said, putting the emphasis on the critical word.

'Fiancée,' Lizzie exclaimed. 'Oh, my God. What's he doing? He was meant to marry you. He said you were the only one for him.'

'I know. And I had to brazen it out in front of them all at the Lindara tea party. It was awful. I was beside myself.' I went on to tell her about letting the pigs out, but only after getting her to promise she would never breathe a word of it to anyone.

'No chance,' she said, as she roared with laughter. 'Good for you. At least you got your own back on him.'

It felt so good to talk it out and gather my thoughts about the situation. It only helped temporarily, though, and as soon as I was on my own again the pain of betrayal haunted me. What was I going to do now that my plans had been thwarted? I had no idea how to move forward.

Lizzie had finished school for the summer, and the next week was full of excursions and visits. We went shopping in the city centre and had walks in the Botanic Gardens and at Shaw's Bridge. We also spent an afternoon in the Ulster Museum. There was a day trip to Bangor on the train and soirées with friends of Lizzie and George. Everyone made me welcome and most of them were like old friends, as I had met them regularly over the years.

One day we went to walk on the steep slopes of Cave Hill, overlooking Belfast Lough and the shipyards, from where we could see the huge hulk of a ship under construction. It was said to be the largest and most luxurious in the world. It was due to be launched in less than two years' time for the trans-atlantic route, and already there was great demand for places on the maiden voyage. We did not know then that it would be named *Titanic*, and would go on to become one of the worst maritime casualties of all time, when it sank in the North Atlantic in April 1912.

We walked into the grounds of Queen's University on another of our excursions, and I stopped to gaze at the hand-some red-brick building with its high windows and central tower. For the first time in my life I imagined what it might be like to study there and I knew it would suit me absolutely. I had always loved academic subjects, yet there was never any thought of continuing my education. Father was not in favour of educating women, and Hannah and I had accepted his view without question.

We went through the large front door into the high-arched entrance hall with its grand gallery and black-and-white chequered flooring. As we passed through into the cloisters Lizzie said,

'Of course, I'll be coming here next year if all goes well with my exams.'

I looked at her in surprise.

'What? You're going to university? I didn't know that.'

'Yes. All being well, I'll be able to study medicine.'

'Oh, my goodness, Lizzie. You're planning to be a doctor? When did you decide to do that?'

'I wanted to go to university, but I didn't know what to study. My sciences are all good and my form teacher suggested it. She's a suffragette, and she is all for women getting an education and the vote. She has been so helpful, and my parents really respect her.'

'Well, all I can say is that you live in a different world. I love my father, but he would never allow me to go to university, never mind encouraging me.'

Lizzie smiled and turned to me.

'I know. Uncle is incredibly old-fashioned and your mother, much as I love her, is just the same. Sorry to say this, but you have no chance of breaking away.'

I knew she was right, but I felt a spike of anger at my

situation. I had the best marks in mathematics and other academic subjects in school, and the worst marks in things like cookery and sewing, yet there had never been any encouragement to further my education.

'Well, while you have been at Methodist College learning all this useful stuff, I have been at Miss Carlisle's School for Young Ladies learning how to set a table and which way to pass the port.'

We roared with laughter at the incongruity of it.

'But you could still go back and do exams and get to university. You have always been clever,' Lizzie said.

'Cleverer than you,' I shot back.

'Well, do something about it then, Miss Smarty-Pants,' she said, and she gave me a gentle shove.

'The truth is that I never considered going further with my education because I thought I would marry Hugh. The stuff I was taught at Miss Carlisle's was right and useful for that world, but look where it has got me now. I have nothing to fall back on.'

The words were said lightly, and I was adept at mocking myself in front of Lizzie, but I knew it was the truth. My whole future had been planned as Hugh's wife, and I was not prepared for the alternative that had suddenly been presented to me the previous Saturday afternoon.

'I know what we'll do,' Lizzie said. 'I'm going to take you to a meeting, and you will see what women are managing to do. It really will inspire you. Mother and I are involved with the movement.' She then realised I didn't know what she was talking about and added, 'The suffragettes. You must come with us to a meeting.'

Aunt B's kind and loving nature had led to her raise money for a children's hospital on Dublin Road. She could not resist going into the clinics and helping with the children and, through her work there, she gained as much competence and knowledge as any qualified nurse. She became a member of the hospital board, working closely with the senior staff, and among them was one of the first women to qualify as a doctor in Ireland. The lady doctor was one of the leaders of the local suffragette movement, and Aunt B had become involved with the group at an early stage.

We went the next evening to Great Victoria Street, where the meeting was being held in the front room of a large town house. I was very curious about the movement and the women involved, but they were not quite what I expected.

'They're all a bit dowdy, aren't they?' I whispered to Lizzie as the meeting started.

She gave me a bemused look and said,

'Well, they have more important things on their mind than clothes and hairstyles. It's not a fashion show, you idiot.'

I had been put in my place. I sat still and concentrated on what was being discussed, determined to learn from the experience.

It was obvious immediately that these were women of substance, who were all educated and working in a wide range of fields – medicine, teaching, business and the trade unions – and I was struck by their self-confidence and knowledge. Every one of them was passionate about the cause and was willing to get involved in the debate of the evening. Aunt B and Lizzie were comfortable in their presence and took part in the discussion, while I listened intently and made sure to miss nothing.

I was impressed with the arguments and was totally convinced that their demands were justified. There were local women, both Catholic and Protestant, an outspoken lady with a broad Scottish accent, numerous ladies with the soft brogue of the south, and all of them were working together for the right to vote. It was an inspiring and eye-opening evening for me. The final words that night found a little place in my heart and lodged there.

'The possession of the franchise is an absolute necessity. Women want to do their duty and fight for their rights with the same weapons as the men.'

Lizzie and I talked half the night. I was now sure that I wanted to continue my education, go to university, and become like the women of the movement. Aunt B encouraged me, but we both knew that it would be a difficult task to persuade Father to let me.

'He's very old-fashioned and stubborn, so you will have to find a way to get round him,' she said. 'I'll do what I can for you, but it won't be easy.'

Lizzie arranged for us to see her teacher, Miss Blakeley, one afternoon, and she advised me on the courses I would need to do and the exams I would need to take before applying to university.

'You will have a lot of hard work to do to catch up,' she warned me, 'but, if you set your mind to it, you can achieve all you wish for.' Once we had discussed it, the way forward became clear and a plan crystallised in my mind.

At the end of the second week I set off home, and Lizzie and Aunt B said goodbye with hugs and kisses and tears. On the train I planned carefully what I would say to Father and the arguments I would present to him. I had to time my talk with him carefully and get him in a good mood.

By the time I had returned, Hugh and Lucinda had gone off to visit relatives in Dublin, but Mother and Hannah could talk of nothing else. I had to listen to endless stories about what Lucinda wore, what she said and how much she loved Lindara. It was midweek before I managed to escape from the house and accompany Father on one of his visits to see a client in Armagh. He was studying papers on the way there, so I knew I had to bide my time. I braced myself for opening the discussion on the way back.

'Did you know Lizzie is going to university next year to become a doctor?' I asked casually.

'Really? What on earth is she doing that for?'

'She was encouraged to do it by a mistress at the school, and Aunt B and Uncle are absolutely behind her. They think it's a great idea.'

'That sister of mine has always had her head in the clouds.'

We were quiet for a minute and then I put the proposition to him. He did not say anything for a moment, and I dared to hope that maybe he would see it from my point of view and give his permission. I was wrong.

'No daughter of mine is going to university. You will marry well and raise children, as is expected of you. Now that is the end of the matter.'

Chapter 7

MARRIAGE

I was in a black mood for what seemed like weeks afterwards. My temperament was in turn crabby then sullen with the family, and for the first week after my return from Belfast I barely ventured out of my room except for meals. When we sat down to eat, I had to listen to all the gossip about Hugh and Lucinda, which Mother felt the need to pass on. It was Hugh this and Lucinda that.

It left me wondering if my mother had any wits about her at all. Sometimes her understanding of me was so limited that I doubted that we were of the same flesh and blood. She and I seemed to inhabit different worlds. The family never enquired why I was in a mood, as that was our way. If someone was upset, it was our practice to leave them alone and then let them come around in their own time, so even Hannah never broached the subject of Hugh with me.

One afternoon, I went wandering in the woods of the Clanhugh estate. Everywhere I looked reminded me of things that Hugh and I had done together, and I found it strangely soothing. I was engrossed in my own world, barely aware of my surroundings, when I heard a peal of laughter and looked up to see Hugh and Lucinda in the distance.

I couldn't bear to meet them and hid down in the laurels, waiting for them to pass. They walked so slowly, hand and hand, smiling and laughing, and it seemed to take forever before they came alongside me. Then they stopped and chatted while I waited, barely able to breathe and afraid to move in case a twig would snap. I was rigid with embarrassment at the thought of them seeing me and believing I was spying on them, and on the way home I decided that I had to find something else to fill my time and take my mind off Hugh.

When I arrived home, Theo Grey was taking tea with my parents and I was called into the drawing room to say hello. Out of courtesy, I asked him about Samuel. He replied,

'He's fine, thank you, and doing really well at school except for his mathematics. He's top of the class in all his other subjects, but for some reason he can't manage the sums.'

'I'll give him some tuition, if you like.' The words were out of my mouth before I had time to think.

'Oh, that would be most kind of you, Sarah,' Theo replied. 'He won't be too keen to spend his summer holidays doing homework, but you can make sure he gets down to it. It would stand him in much better stead for next year.'

'I'll call tomorrow and see him,' I said, and with that the matter was settled. Looking back, it seems as if that one impetuous moment took my life in a new direction and, from then on, things fell into place like a line of collapsing dominoes.

Was it just chance that Theo was visiting my parents that day? Most of the business he had with my father was conducted in his office or at the hotel, so he was not a regular visitor to the house during the working day. Yet his presence that day had great importance for my future. Who knows if it was fate or serendipity? I have never been able to decide which.

I walked into Lindara the next morning and found Samuel waiting for me at the door of the hotel where he and Theo lived. We went to the dining room and I saw that he had already set out his books. He was shy with me at first, but we soon fell into easy conversation as he told me about school in Enniskillen.

'Let's make a start,' I suggested. 'We will do a few exercises so that I can see what you are having problems with.'

We went over some of his work and I realised immediately that he hadn't grasped the basics of algebra. We worked together that day and every morning for the next two weeks. He was a clever boy with a quick brain and, once I had worked out that he needed to go back over the foundations of the algebra course, he made rapid progress. Towards the end of the second week Theo popped into the dining room to ask how he was getting on.

'Really well,' I said. 'He will be up to scratch by the time he goes back to school.' Then, as an afterthought, I added, 'If I were you, I'd ask for a refund on the fees from Samuel's school.'

'Why's that?'

'There is nothing wrong with Samuel's ability. He just had a very bad maths teacher. You should expect more from a school charging such high fees, and I think you deserve a refund.'

Theo threw back his head and laughed, and when he did the years seemed to roll off him. I glimpsed a younger, more vibrant Theo, with an attractive sense of fun.

'You would make a fine businesswoman, Sarah. You should think about using that brain of yours.'

I have often wondered if that remark planted a seed in both our minds. Did he already see in me the businesswoman and partner he was looking for? I know I caught his interest for the first time, and I realised there was much more to Theo than I had previously thought.

Somehow, that first fleeting attraction to his personality grew, and I found myself wondering about him and looking for him when I went to the hotel. Perhaps it was what I needed to get over Hugh. In those few short weeks something clicked in both our minds and we circled each other in the early stages of courtship.

Theo and I were married the following October, four months after the Pig Tea Party. It caused a storm, as I knew it would. Mother, Father and Hannah were shocked at the news and Hannah took to her bed for three days in tears, while I brazened it out as best I could.

It hadn't been difficult to arouse Theo's interest. He had been a widower for many years, since his wife died in childbirth and he was left with his son, his business and his political interests. It was so easy to invent reasons to see him or to be wherever he was and offer help. A cordial relationship quickly grew into a warm one and, with gentle manipulation from me, it became, on his part, desire. I could see it in his eyes, and I knew that I had succeeded in ousting Hannah from his affections.

It was for the best. She could never have managed to take care of Theo's business interests the way I did, and I told her she would be much happier with William Montgomery, who'd had his eye on her since childhood. Her marriage to him and the subsequent years of devotion proved me right, but she didn't thank me at the time.

Hugh was married the following summer in a high society wedding in Yorkshire, where Lucinda's parents had their ancestral home. We heard all about it in detail from Lady Clanhugh, who was overawed by the grandeur of Lucinda's family.

It was the first time I was made aware of the hierarchy and petty divisions in the aristocracy. Lord Clanhugh was at the top of the local society in Ulster, and with his seat in the House of Lords and his home in London, he was also at the pinnacle of English society. So, it was with some surprise that I learnt that there were those in England who thought they were better than the Clanhughs. Lucinda's family were very wealthy and, added to this, her mother was related to the royal family, a fact that seemed to intimidate Lady Clanhugh and increase the pressure as she prepared for the wedding.

The couple married. Then, after an extended honeymoon touring Europe, they settled in London, where Hugh took up a job in the city. From what we heard, they lived the high life in the capital, mixing with the cream of society, including the fast set around the young royals. They visited Lindara infrequently during the first year of their marriage and, when they did, they stayed no more than a week.

I found it difficult to understand how Hugh had changed so much under his wife's influence. He had always adored Lindara and spent as much time there as possible, but since his marriage to Lucinda he rarely came back home. I can't say I was sorry, because it meant I did not have the embarrassment of trying to be civil and put on a polite front in their company.

I took a while to find my own niche in my marriage to Theo. Once the honeymoon was over, he quickly settled into a routine of work, political meetings and fishing, while I seemed to impinge very little on his life. Oh, he was fond of me, but any passion for me was quickly satisfied, and within a few months his life was back in the same routine he had had for years. I never found the physical side of our relationship easy. I had grown to respect Theo and wanted to do well by him, but the physique of a sixty-year-old man did not fill me with desire.

My biggest shock was when we returned from our honeymoon in Connemara and I discovered that his only living quarters in the hotel were his study and his bedroom.

'Is that it?' I asked cautiously when he showed me round. I had imagined one or maybe two reception rooms, which we could use and where we could entertain our friends, but there were none.

'Sure, this is all I need,' he replied, and I could see that it wasn't wise to push him just then. I was already learning to bide my time with Theo, for he had a stubborn streak. It may seem odd that I hadn't been aware of this before we married, but the courtship was not only quick, it was also very correct. Consequently, I hadn't got to know a lot about his private life before we married.

His study was a revelation to me. There was an easy chair drawn up by the fire, with the table alongside for his drinks, pipe, tobacco and magazines. In one corner there was a table and four chairs, which he obviously used for his political meetings, as it was piled high with reports and minutes. A bureau lay open with correspondence waiting to be attended to, and the other half of the room was full of the clutter of fishing gear – rods, nets, spinners, fly-tying equipment, and a bank of little boxes made up of drawers to hold the flies, leads and hooks. It was completely and utterly a man's room.

He must have seen the look of horror on my face when he showed me the room because he turned to me and said,

'Now, you're not to touch this room, Sarah. I know exactly where everything is, and I like it that way. You're not to go tidying up, do you hear?'

His bedroom, by contrast, was neat and tidy, if a bit bare. When I moved into the hotel, it was the only room which was private to me, and even then, it was not for my exclusive use. I persuaded Theo to allow me to convert one of the small bedrooms into a sitting room for my own use, and that really was the start of it.

The fun I had decorating and furnishing the room to a strict budget gave me the impetus to carry on and refurbish the rest of the hotel. Theo took some persuading, but I realised that the way to get through to him was to make the argument on financial terms, so that's exactly what I did. He agreed that I could work on one room at a time, on a very limited budget. I found very quickly that I could haggle for the best rates with the local businessmen if they thought there was a lot more work up the line. I enjoyed dealing with them, beating the price down and getting the earliest completion date. It was my first taste of real power, and as I slowly proved myself Theo's confidence in me grew.

One morning, after I had left the accounts for him to look at, he came into the kitchen, leant over in front of the cook, Violet, and Samuel, and kissed me.

'What a clever wife I've got, Violet. She's a girl and a half, aren't you, Sarah?'

We all laughed at him, as it was so out of character for Theo to be demonstrative. Samuel was particularly pleased to see his father happy and he chuckled to himself. I winked at him, knowing that he would tease me about it later, because he and I now had a very easy relationship. He had never known his mother, and he was glad to have a woman around to talk to. I was near his age and took an interest in his friends and his hobbies, so we were almost like brother and sister.

At that time, Samuel and I were both learning to drive. We spent the early evenings out in Theo's car on the country roads around Lindara. We used the three-mile route that took us out of town to the crossroads at the Black Bog and back again on the road past the mill. The roads were very poor, and the car had little suspension, so we had a lot of very bumpy rides, but, by the time we had done it a few times, we knew every pothole.

I was first to learn, so Samuel got the job of turning the crank handle to start the engine, then he would jump in while I steered us out of the yard and onto the main road. I got the hang of it in no time and I loved the thrill of it right away. There were only a few cars on the roads, and even fewer woman drivers, so I must have been one of the first lady drivers in the country. Of all the things I achieved in my life, learning to drive that car was one of the most pleasurable.

Samuel took a bit longer to advance than me, but then he was young and didn't have the same aptitude. He was very hard on himself when he got things wrong, but I just laughed it off and told him to try again. He soon built up confidence and mastered the art of motoring.

We had such fun on those summer evenings, with the windows of the car wide open and the wind blowing my hair in a stream behind me. It was then, as he got to know me, that Samuel slowly opened up. He told me about his time at school and his life before I knew him, and we became firm friends. I remember thinking that with my new husband, the hotel to run, Samuel as a friend and the delights of driving, I had everything I needed.

The other important catalyst for me was a visit to the village of one of the McCauley girls. She arrived from New York the summer after we were married on a visit to her family. The McCauleys were a decent enough family, but they never had two pennies to rub together. Yet Mona arrived home with the latest fashion money could buy. She even stayed at the hotel, claiming that there wasn't enough room in the family house. She thought nothing of hiring a car to come all the way from Armagh to take her and her mother off round the country visiting relatives. The whole village was proud of the local girl made good.

'Did you see Mona Macauley's coat?' Hannah asked, when she saw her in the hotel dining room one day. 'It must have cost a fortune.' I couldn't help going through to have a peek. Hannah and I both loved fashion and we shopped every month in Armagh and Portadown for the latest trends, so I was keen to see Mona's coat almost as much as I was keen to have a good look at her.

I was fascinated by her. She had her own business in New York, hiring out Irish immigrants into service in the big houses and hotels that needed them. On the back of hard work and a good idea she'd made a mountain of money. What's more, she'd done it on her own, without backing or help from any man. I contrasted her position guiltily with my own. There is no doubt that I'd married the money, but at least I now had a way to prove to myself that I could also make money and be a success.

The refurbishment of the hotel went ahead as scheduled, but I knew we needed more than just decor to make a mark.

I found the answer right under my nose. Violet, our cook, proved to be a real treasure. She was running the hotel before I married Theo and I had been aware that I didn't want to make an enemy of her. She was polite and courteous with me, but I sensed a reserve in her, and I knew that I was being judged. She had worked for a wealthy family with homes in Ireland and in London and had an excellent reputation as a cook, so it was obvious that she would have no trouble finding work elsewhere if we didn't get along.

Violet had a natural authority with the housemaids and waiters, and I realised very quickly that it was best to leave things as they were and let her continue to run the kitchen and household staff. That would give me time to concentrate on the things I enjoyed doing, which were organising the refurbishment and controlling the books. She could see that I was making changes and improvements, and she came to me with her cookbooks and a collection of recipes that her sister used in another grand home.

'What about trying a few of these recipes?' she suggested, flicking through the book. 'They always went down a treat with the Granbys.' She was keen to experiment and to provide more adventurous food in the hotel.

Her idea was a great success. Within no time the reputation of the Lindara Hotel spread, and we found that more and more people were prepared to travel the extra miles to stay with us. The whole place changed from a sleepy, small hotel with basic food and accommodation, to become a place that people would journey to, just to eat and drink.

We were all drawn into the excitement of seeing a small business grow and become successful, and as Violet and I worked together she dropped her reserve and we worked as partners. Theo was delighted with me and I was rather pleased with myself.

The thing that capped it all was the music that the O'Connells played in the bar of the hotel on a Saturday night. They were a big extended Catholic family that numbered half the village, and most of them worked at the mill – the ones who stayed at home that is, and didn't emigrate to England, America or Australia. There was a whole tribe of them, brothers and sisters, children and grandchildren, and you could tell an O'Connell at a glance.

They came in two breeds: the good-looking ones, who were tall and lean with dark, curly hair and the clear blue eyes of the pure Celt, and the redheaded O'Connells, who were wee and stumpy, with ginger hair and freckles and a touch of the halfwit about them. All of them had a great love of traditional Irish music. They had music in their bones and every one of them played an instrument, even Billy, who played the spoons with a flourish. The young lass Teresa used to sing, and she had the voice of an angel.

I would help in the bar on the nights they played, for I loved the music. I'd longed to play the fiddle as a child, but my mother wouldn't hear of it, making me learn the piano instead, but it never set my heart racing and my foot tapping like the sound of a fiddle playing an Irish jig. When the O'Connells were playing their music, the bar would fill up until you couldn't move. Big fellows, both Catholic and Protestant, would come from miles around to listen and sup a pint of Guinness on a Saturday night after the week's work was done.

Samuel always managed to sneak in and make himself useful about the place so that he could listen too. My greatest pleasure was standing at the end of the bar, the place packed and the music playing, a big fire burning in the grate and a glass of Bushmills in my hand. I thought it was grand, not only for the music but for the business it brought in, but I knew that Theo never really liked me down there with the locals. He thought it was no place for his wife, but I suspected there was more to it than his idea of my social station. He was evasive when I questioned him, and mumbled,

'They are ones to watch, the O'Connells.'

'What do you mean by that?' I asked, but he only repeated his comment with a dark look in his eye and said no more. I never understood what he had against them because, after all, most of them worked in his mill. If they were trouble or 'ones to watch', as he put it, why did he employ them?

So I chose to ignore his words of warning. Instead, I held the sentiment of that scene in my heart, delighting in the bond that arose from the shared love of music, thinking that there was hope for us all if only we could extend the ease of friendship throughout the rest of the week.

By the middle of 1912 the Lindara Hotel was firmly on the map in West Armagh. That summer, political events developed rapidly. The possibility of home rule, which had hung over us for a long time, became a real threat, and the Protestants began to organise against it. Theo had been in the thick of it for some time, along with Lord Clanhugh, and although we didn't discuss it much he dropped snippets of information to me.

I knew that the Protestants would never accept the Home Rule Bill. The meetings, the money-raising and the organisation were well under way.

And although I knew that Theo was involved in the organisation, I did not fully appreciate just how important he was until September of that year. That was when I finally realised that he was in the inner circle at the very top of the organisation that was opposing home rule.

Chapter 8

HOME RULE

My knowledge of Theo's activities was limited because I tended to steer clear of discussing politics with him. I knew we would disagree. I simply avoided the subject, preferring to talk about Samuel, fishing, the hotel and his business. I had argued long and hard with my father, to the extent that it had damaged the close relationship I had always had with him – so I knew that I had to find a way of living with the people I loved, while accepting that we had a difference of opinion on matters of importance that would affect all our lives.

The relationship between the rest of the family and me was troubled for some time after my marriage, given what I had done to Hannah. It was hard for them to forgive me, and I couldn't really blame them. Even though we were on speaking terms, there was a coldness between us, particularly between Mother and me. She was the least ready to pardon my actions. Mother had always been closest to Hannah, just as Father had always had more time for me.

Hannah and Mother shared a love of all things domestic. They both adored cooking, baking, sewing, making the home beautiful and entertaining, and they never needed anything beyond that. They were often in the kitchen working together, creating new recipes or experimenting with old favourites, or baking scones and cakes for the church supper. There was an atmosphere of peace and tranquillity when they worked together. I would go into the kitchen and find them chatting easily, each doing their own job without any need to confer. They worked together naturally as a team.

Hannah had slowly softened towards me, partly because she was curious to find out about my life in the hotel, and also because once I started renovating it she was always eager to travel with me to Armagh or Belfast to look for furnishings. She loved being involved with flicking through swatches of sample books and choosing the materials. As she grew more interested, her good nature returned and we were friends again. She had missed our clothes shopping expeditions too, and we were both glad that the rift between us was gone and we could enjoy each other's company again. Then, in the spring, William Montgomery started to come courting her and romance developed quickly. Hannah blossomed with his attention and, in time, it was easy to see that they would make the perfect match. Even Mother was happy, and she mellowed towards me slightly.

In contrast to Hannah and Mother, I was only interested in the world beyond the domestic sphere. I used to seek out my father so that I could question him about people and places, and all the things that I didn't understand but wanted to know about. Even as a child it was his company that I wanted.

'Can I come?' I asked, as soon as he put his coat on. I loved nothing better than to go with him on business and see the places he visited. Factories, mills, offices and places of work were all fascinating to me. Father would always answer my questions and talk to me about his work and his clients, and it was with his help and guidance that I began to understand the political issues of the day. Whether it was youth, or a sense of justice, or just the rebel in me, I'm not sure, but I began to take my own independent line on many of the current issues.

The first thing we rowed about was the suffragettes. In 1911 they began to get a great deal of coverage in the newspapers because of their bold, headline-grabbing stunts. I supported them wholeheartedly, praising their actions and arguing for their cause. Father was more cautious and, whatever he felt about their aims, he could not bring himself to support their 'mad antics', as he called them. I followed their campaign closely and was excited by the acts of defiance and the hunger strikes they undertook in prison, but Father was an old-fashioned man and he couldn't see the point in giving votes to women.

I grew more radical. And, as I did, Father seemed to grow more conservative. Talking about the suffragettes in England was one thing. Arguing about Irish politics was much more emotional, yet it was difficult for us to avoid the big issue, which was home rule. We disagreed vehemently when the first big rally took place at James Craig's house, Craigavon, on the banks of Belfast Lough. Sir Edward Carson, the barrister from Dublin, addressed a crowd of fifty thousand that autumn day in 1911, encouraging them to prepare for the government of the Protestant province of Ulster. It was a rabble-rousing speech that led to the setting up of the military wing of the home rule movement, which became known as the Ulster Volunteer Force. It was supported by most, but not all, of the prominent Protestants in Ulster.

'What sort of girl are you, that you can't see the sense of it?' my father asked when we argued.

'I just don't think that dividing Ireland is the answer,' I replied, holding steadfastly to my views.

'What does a slip of a girl like you know anyway?' he asked in exasperation.

I sighed and held myself back from saying, yet again,

'I'm not a slip of a girl any more. I'm a married woman.' Instead I ignored his remarks and continued to spar with him. 'I'm not alone in what I think. I'm in some fairly heavyweight company.'

'Oh, you're deluding yourself there, my girl.'

'And are Sir Roger Casement and Lord Pirrie deluding themselves as well?' I asked facetiously.

It was my attitude that seemed to upset him most, my ability to answer back, to think for myself and even to be flippant about matters that were of great concern to him. At that time, there were still Protestants who questioned the wisdom of Ireland being divided, and they included men of very high standing. Yet, it was as if the whole province was being carried away with the stirring speeches of Carson, who led the opposition to home rule.

In 1912, more rallies were held across Ulster and trouble slowly brewed. My worst fears were confirmed during the season of Orange marches, when the whole of Ulster seemed to go a little bit mad.

In Castledawson in late June, there was a clash between a Sunday school outing that was marching with bands and banners under the Union Jack, and a procession of the Ancient Order of Hibernians. Several children were badly hurt, and it provoked a backlash by the workers in the Belfast shipyards.

Shipbuilding was one of the biggest and most important industries in Belfast, but there had always been deep hatred in the shipyards. Most of the workers were from Protestant enclaves and they held the upper hand. On the Monday after Castledawson, they turned on their Catholic workmates, calling for the expulsion of all Fenians and Home Rulers. In the violence and intimidation that followed, some two thousand workers were forced out of their jobs.

'Is that what you wanted?' I chided my father as I read the news.

'The lads in the shipyard were provoked by those ones at Castledawson,' he replied. Neither of us could see the other's point of view, yet we couldn't seem to hold our tongues and stop the constant bickering

'Will you stop, you two?' my mother said, exasperated with both of us. 'I don't want to hear another word about it from either of you.'

So we sat in silence, or else changed the subject and tried to talk of things that were neutral.

Hannah scolded me when we were alone.

'Just learn to hold your tongue, Sarah,' she said in a kindly way, trying to make me the image of herself. 'It's easier that way. Honestly. Just try it and you'll see.'

'But why should I hold my tongue? I have views and I have the right to express them. How will I ever influence Father or make him see sense if I don't show him another point of view?'

Hannah sighed at my intransigence.

'You're never going to change him, Sarah. You're wasting your breath, if that's what you think. And you're giving Mother and me headaches into the bargain. We are fed up with both of you.'

I tried to hold back and avoid any unpleasantness. Eventually I found that it was easier not to go home so often, but that was very difficult for me. Father and I had always been close, but now we could barely sit together in the same room. Gradually, I moved away from them and became my own woman.

I can see now that it must have been difficult for Father because he was a man of his era, a patriarch accustomed to having his own way, unused to being challenged – and I was wild and headstrong compared to girls of the time. It was as if I had a man's brain in a woman's body.

Life was so much easier and predictable for Hannah, who wanted everything that our parents expected of her – but although things were harder for me, I never envied her equanimity. Her life always seemed dull compared to mine.

In September 1912, the Anti-Home Rule movement organised a programme of rallies throughout the province. They started in Enniskillen and swept across the six counties holding meetings as they went, with Carson as the main speaker.

It was all to come to a head on Ulster Day, 28 September, when everyone who was against home rule for Ulster was asked to sign the covenant. It caused a great stir. There wasn't a Protestant, man or woman, among all our family and friends who didn't intend signing the covenant that day.

The only one who was determined not to do so was me.

That was when I had my one and only row with Theo.

Chapter 9

JOHN BROWN

These days the television throws up pictures of violence every night – a bomb in Belfast, a shooting in Londonderry. What has changed in the last sixty years? Ireland is full of hard, unforgiving men on both sides who know only the logic of mutilation and murder. The whole show is run by the bullies from the backstreets, while decent people look on in horror and distance themselves from the violence as much as they can.

It was different in my day. Back then it was the gentry and professional people who organised things, kept things straight. They saw it as the decent thing to do because it was about tradition and defending the Empire, and the show of strength was meant to make the British government think twice about home rule. There was none of this dirty business of bombing and scaring innocent women and children – it was a man's fight.

Even so, from the beginning, I was wary of where the show of strength would lead us. The threat of home rule put the fear of God into most Protestants, but I always had mixed feelings about it. I loved so much about the Irish way of life, particularly the more rural way of life of the south and the west. The people seemed relaxed, unfazed by the modern world, and always had a spare moment to pass the time of day. They liked their drink and their music, and they knew how to enjoy themselves. It always contrasted so strongly with the prissy Presbyterianism that seemed to dominate our lives in the north. We seemed so judgemental in comparison. There was too much duty and so much less of the sheer enjoyment of life in us.

That was only one side of it, though, as I knew how the priests could dominate and rule their Catholic flock, and they did so with a harshness that crossed into cruelty at times. I have no respect for the domination of the church in state affairs, and I knew the critics were right when they said the Catholic Church would impose its will on us in an independent United Ireland.

Yet, I have to say that I felt more akin to my Irish countrymen than I did to the English. The only English people we came across in Ireland were men of power, the men who ran things, the men who ruled.

I remember the feeling of amazement when, at the age of sixteen, I met a great uncouth lump of a woman and realised she was English. The only English women I'd known were upper-class and I'd thought that all English women were grand, that they dressed well, took tea at four, dinner at eight, ran a house with a bevy of servants, had nannies, horses and were cultured. I thought that was what all the English were like.

We were like a colony for England, and had a relationship and a mentality that was colonial. It gave us an inbred sense of inferiority, just as it gave them their God-given superiority. With our Irish brothers we were at least one and the same.

'You're going to sign the covenant, I take it, Sarah?' Theo enquired one day in September 1912. I hesitated, unwilling to lie and yet not wanting to risk a row. 'I have arranged for you to be picked up for the signing,' Theo said, peering over the top of his newspaper.

I was silent for a moment, choosing my words carefully before I answered.

'No, I'm not going to,' I said slowly. 'What exactly have you arranged?'

He must have heard the slight edge in my voice, for he lowered his paper and looked at me over the rims of his half-moon glasses. He folded the paper and set it down on the breakfast table.

'Willie will drive you, your mother and Hannah to Armagh for the signing of the Woman's Declaration, a parallel document for women. He will call for you at nine o'clock sharp. I'll be up in Belfast for the big rally,' he explained, as he spread marmalade on his toast.

'Why have you done that, Theo?' I asked carefully. 'You know my thoughts on the subject.'

'We need your support, Sarah,' he said briskly, as if the question was closed.

'Theo, you know how I feel about this issue. I'm not happy to sign,' I said, my voice rising slightly.

'We need to protect our interests, Sarah. Just look around you. Do you think we'll manage to live the same lifestyle if we become part of the Free State with all their economic problems? No. We'll just end up subsidising the rest of Ireland.'

'I know how you feel about that,' I said, hoping to stem the argument that was brewing.

'Ulster is by far the most industrialised province, and will stay that way. We need foreign markets for our growth, and we can only be assured of keeping our access to those markets if we remain a part of Britain.'

I knew all the arguments and had heard them a hundred times. I was more worried about the small, everyday effects of the division of Ireland. Lindara sat almost on the border of Armagh and Monaghan and, if Ireland was divided, the border would go along the county line. It was unthinkable that we could be entering a foreign country just by going a mile out of the village down some country lane. What about our workers? Would our mill hands still be able to work for us if they had to enter a different country every morning to earn a wage?

I knew I should have left it there, but it was important to both of us and we just couldn't manage to agree on it. Theo was a traditionalist, and he couldn't for the life of him see why anyone would support the disintegration of the Empire. Indeed, he felt that the politicians at Westminster who agreed with home rule were the real traitors, not the Ulster Protestants. I understood both sides, but in my heart of hearts I could not support a divided Ireland.

The row was serious for both of us and neither of us would back down. In the end he could not get the better of me. He sighed and gathered his thoughts for a minute while I stood there, unsure of what was coming.

'Well, Sarah,' he said. 'I can see that I'm not going to turn you. No amount of argument or persuasion or even ordering will change your mind.' He moved over beside me then and put his hands on my shoulders, looking me straight in the eye, and, controlling the anger in his voice, said,

'Do what you will. Keep what views you have but promise me one thing – that you will never publicly undermine my position. That would be more than I could tolerate. Just promise me, Sarah, that whatever you do, you'll do it in private and not stand against me in public.'

It was not difficult to make the promise, for I had no intentions of becoming a suffragette or a rabble-rouser. I had no desire to make a fool of Theo. I only wanted to be allowed to have my own opinions and to live by them.

On Ulster Day, the rest of the family all turned out to sign the covenant. I was probably the only Protestant left in Lindara but, true to my word, I spent the day indoors getting on with jobs. They came home full of it, but little was said about my not being there. I think the whole family had given up on me by that stage.

In all, 218,206 men signed the covenant and 228,991 women signed the declaration, a total of almost half a million people. In the cities of Britain, a further 24,217 Ulster men and women signed. It was an impressive show of solidarity.

In the coming months Theo took on more responsibility for fundraising, which meant he was away much of the time in Belfast and all over the province. His role was that of trusted banker for the movement, and he was the person who controlled the funds. His reputation was so clean that it was beyond question.

It was then that I first heard the name John Brown.

'I think we have found ourselves a bit of a boyo,' Theo said one evening.

'What do you mean?' I asked.

'Young fellow from outside Portadown. Knows a thing or two about getting hardware for the movement.'

'So, how did you come across him?'

'Through Alex Shaw over at Portadown. He funded one or two of the small trial runs for him, and the fellow has come up good. He has been giving him more responsibility each time and he has come through with the goods. In record time as well.'

'Sounds like just the man you need,' I replied, and already the description of him fascinated me.

John burst into our lives that winter like a comet on the rise. Born and raised in Carrick, south of Portadown, his family were farmers, but they were a cut above the normal labouring farmers for the whole family were a brainy lot. It was said that they had an air about them that set them apart. They had no more money than their neighbours, but they all had a striving mind, the will for self-education and the drive to get on in the world.

John had the knack of knowing how things were going ahead of time and, for this reason he started one of the first gun clubs in the province. He saw that if it came to a show of strength, men needed to be trained in the use of weapons in order to put up a viable resistance to home rule. They needed guns and his first act of procurement became the stuff of legend, but I heard it from his own lips and all of it was true.

He started his career as arms procurer in a typically maverick fashion. One Sunday he was stung into action by the ribbing of one of the men. They only had one or two guns between them, and the men spent more of their time waiting their turn than training. One of the young bucks remarked,

'After a long day's engagement the South Armagh division routed the enemy with their wooden rifles and suffered no casualties.' It was only a jape, but John felt it deeply and next morning he sought an interview with his employer, Alex Shaw, a wealthy local businessman who was a stout supporter of the cause.

With a bag full of money, he set off to Belfast and took the overnight boat to Liverpool. He went by train to Birmingham, where he had connections, and there he managed to buy a selection of weapons from one of the many small arms manufacturers in the city. By late afternoon he was on the train to Liverpool to catch the boat back to Belfast, the empty suitcases he had taken with him full of guns. His friend on the ship got him into a cabin for the night and helped to smuggle the cases off the next morning among other luggage. By early afternoon he was back in Portadown with weapons ready for use at the gun club's midweek meeting.

That trip set him on his career as a procurer and gunrunner for the UVF, the Ulster Volunteer Force. He proved himself trustworthy, and he was quickly accepted into the inner circle and entrusted with jobs of great secrecy. He travelled extensively in Europe, for it was there, in the large foundries of Germany and Belgium, that the best deals were done. He slipped in and out of the country and there was always an air of mystery and slight menace about him, which he played up to. It suited him very well to be his own master and to be answerable only to the men who paid his large fees. He did not like to be asked too much about where he was going or what he was doing, for in that way he could ply his trade and keep his business to himself.

I heard these stories about John for at least a year before I met him. He came to the hotel or to Lindara, but he came for meetings only and then he was gone. He never had time to stop for a drink or chat, and I only managed to get a glimpse of him as he was going out the door. I did note that he always wore an expensive loden coat, and I saw then that he was a man of taste who knew how to make money and how to spend it. By the time I was finally introduced to him I was agog with curiosity.

John Brown had charm in abundance. It danced in his eyes when we met, and he looked at me and said in his slow drawl,

'So very pleased to meet you, Mrs Grey. I hope I have not deprived you of your husband's company too much of late. I'm afraid the call of duty has us all working far too hard.'

He was tall, with a broad, athletic build and dark brown hair, but it was his eyes that were unforgettable. I was thoroughly taken with him – but then we all were. He filled a room when he was in it, drawing all the light and energy into him like the centrepiece of a Rembrandt painting. He put everyone else in the shadow, yet he seemed to do it unwittingly. He was never fully aware of the aura he brought with him.

Samuel became his shadow when he was in Lindara – he adored John and you could see why. Samuel was close to Theo, but the relationship was a quiet, relaxed one based on their common love of fishing. John had all the dash and excitement that his old father lacked. Theo was the solid, sensible citizen, while John was a maverick entrepreneur, who blew in from nowhere and immediately set the place buzzing.

In the summer of 1913, Hugh and Lucinda returned to live in Lindara, to run the estate in the absence of Hugh's father. Lord Clanhugh had decided that he needed to be in London for most of the time, to exercise influence in the House of

Lords. The pressure for home rule was growing from the Irish nationalists, who held the balance of power, and he needed to spend as much time in Westminster as possible, cajoling his parliamentary colleagues.

It therefore fell to Hugh and Lucinda to help with the organisation of the local branch of the Ulster Volunteer Force. Despite Theo's role as banker for the movement, I refused to have anything to do with it.

I was adamant that I would take no part in anything political, no matter how much pressure I came under to do so, but in truth it gave me an excuse to stay well out of Lucinda's way. I could not stand being in her company, in part because a bit of me was still smarting from Hugh's rejection, but also because I found her high-handed and unfriendly.

I kept my distance from both of them.

Chapter 10

THE TRAINING CAMPS

In the autumn of 1913, training camps for the newly formed Ulster Volunteer Force were being run on many of the large estates in Ulster. The local branch proposed a series of one-week camps at Lindara, so Hugh and Lucinda threw themselves into the organisation.

I was asked to arrange the food supplies and, although I was not prepared to have any political involvement, I could see no good reason not to enter a straightforward business arrangement. They needed to get food from somewhere, and I felt I may as well supply it and do my business some good at the same time, but it pained me to have anything to do with it.

Watching Lucinda running things at Hugh's side was difficult to bear. They were keen to use my suppliers, and to get the best prices for the large quantity of food they needed, so I was summoned to Lindara House to discuss the arrangements. Reluctantly I agreed.

I dressed with great care that morning. I must have pulled out six different outfits to try on before I settled on one. I wanted to look my best and I knew exactly the look I wanted to achieve – businesslike and stylish. Women's fashion was geared towards day dresses for home and more elaborate outfits for going out or entertaining, but I wanted the formality of a man's business suit with the added feminine touches that would show me to be a woman of taste. I managed it with a simple black skirt and a white blouse finished off with silver jewellery made by craftsmen in Armagh. I checked myself carefully in the mirror and felt full of confidence, ready for the meeting with Lucinda.

I always walked, in preference to driving or taking the pony and trap, and I went up the drive to Lindara House on that fine autumn morning with the sun shining, the air fresh and clear, and the trees in their full autumnal glory. It was a joy to be walking in those woods again.

I rarely ventured onto the estate, partly because I was always busy at the hotel, but mostly because of my reluctance to be reminded of Hugh at every turn. Every part of the grounds held some special memory for me – the field where we had raced the ponies, the island in the river where we had made summer camps and baked potatoes on an open fire (though they were always charred on the outside and raw in the middle), the bamboo forest near the kitchen garden that we raided for fishing poles, and the rope swing on the big chestnut tree where we dared each other to go higher.

My fondest memories, the ones I put out of my mind, were of summer days on the bank by the river, far out on the edge of the estate where few ventured, and where we picnicked and talked of our dreams. On still days we used to lie there side by side, content to be together, and watch for the turquoise flash of a kingfisher. That is where we pledged our love for each other, the love he said would last forever only months before he returned to Lindara with Lucinda.

My stomach knotted as I drew near the house. I dreaded

seeing Hugh and Lucinda together because of the way she fussed over him, demonstrating her feminine charms to everyone. I supposed that helpless little-girl allure was what had won his heart. As I braced myself for meeting him I had to admit that, while I neither loved nor hated him now, my feelings for Hugh had not yet reached the comfort of indifference.

Old Bailey was at the door of Lindara House, looking out for me.

'Her ladyship is up at the field. She said to send you on up, Mrs Grey.'

'It's the home farm field they're setting up in, I take it.'

'Aye, that's right. You'll find them up there OK.'

'Thanks, Bailey,' I said, as his gnarled old body retreated into the house.

The walk to the home farm field would put ten minutes onto my journey each way, and I had no time to waste because I was due back at the hotel for another appointment. Lucinda could not have known how she would inconvenience me when she changed the arrangements, but I doubted if she had even considered it. I set off at a brisk pace and walked around the curve of the lake, through the stable yard and down the lane.

The scene before me was like a medieval spectacle. There were lines of tents in bleached canvas and khaki set out in rows around an open square. The autumn colours of the trees were like the banners of jousting teams draped around the field in bright red, orange and brown. In the middle of this, I saw the small figure of Lucinda, with her auburn hair tied on top of her head, giving orders to the men in her fine English accent.

'Sarah,' she said as she caught sight of me. 'So, Bailey sent you over all right?'

'Yes, indeed. He was at the front door waiting for me and directed me down here.'

'Well, do come and sit down, and we can go through the menus and make a list of the food to be ordered. I will be so glad of your advice. I've done most of it with Cook but, to be honest, she and I are only guessing at the quantities involved. You're far more experienced at this than I am, so I would welcome your thoughts on the subject.'

We went through the menus together and I looked at her with a gathering sense of disbelief. She was obviously much more used to feeding gentry than ordinary labouring men.

'This is going to cost you, Lucinda. I doubt that you will cover the cost of these menus with the contributions from the men,' I commented carefully.

'You're right, Sarah, but I want the Lindara training camp to be the best in the province. The men are going to remember our camp.'

'Well, I'm sure you're right, but I don't think you have to break the bank to make it memorable,' I cautioned her. 'Most of the local farm labourers will be perfectly happy with simple fare, you know. A few good stews with plenty of potatoes and vegetables are all they are used to. They won't expect anything fancy.'

Lucinda fixed me with her green eyes and let my comments hang in the air for a moment, as if she needed to think how to reply to someone who had the nerve to question her judgement. She continued to stare at me, and then smiled coolly as she said,

'I want to do things well, Sarah. We will stick with the menus

I have prepared with Cook. So, if you would be so kind as to arrange for the deliveries of the food…'

Her voice had the message that further discussion was not necessary. Lucinda had made up her mind that she wanted more than just to feed the men – she wanted to put on a show. She wanted Lindara to be bigger, better and grander than all the other training camps, and no one was going to dissuade her from that decision. I had tried but, in the end, the decision was hers and I, after all, would make more money from the bigger bills that would be incurred.

'Well, that's that, then. We seem to have sorted it out to your satisfaction,' I said.

'Yes. Thank you for your help, Sarah.'

'Oh, you and Cook seemed to have it all well worked out between you. I don't think I have been much help.'

'Oh, but you have been a great help. You are going to organise all the supplies for us. I don't know what I would have done without you,' she said, the insincerity ringing in her voice. 'Ah, there's Hugh,' she cried, and my head turned to follow her gaze. 'Over here, darling.'

'I really must go,' I said. 'I have to see a man from Armagh about carpet for the dining room. He's due at twelve o'clock.'

'Oh God, Sarah, he's only trade. He can wait,' she exclaimed, turning away from me to greet Hugh, who was walking up the field with John Brown.

Hugh came up and nodded at me, but had eyes only for Lucinda. He put his arm around her waist and kissed her gently on the cheek.

'Hello. So good to see you, Sarah,' he said, barely glancing at me. John and I exchanged greetings. He stood to one side, saying little but not missing a thing.

'Sarah's been so helpful with the arrangements for the food for next week,' Lucinda told Hugh.

'I told you Sarah was the one to get you organised, darling,' he said. 'Sarah is the one with the head for business around here.' He smiled into her eyes.

I stood there feeling like a great gawk. Why was it that Lucinda could always make me feel so inadequate? There she was with her auburn hair, her creamy porcelain skin that was almost transparent, her green eyes and a sprinkling of freckles that danced lightly over her small nose, and without doing a thing she made me feel like a great lump. She was so effortlessly feminine that she made me almost feel mannish.

Everywhere else and with everyone else I was self-confident and at ease. I had always been proud of my height, my straight-backed bearing, my thick black hair and my strong features. People never described me as pretty – it was not a word that applied to my looks and style – but I was called striking and modish, and those were words that I could identify with. But never pretty, and certainly not beautiful. When I was with Lucinda, all the things that I had fought for in my life – my independence, and my need to make my way in the world of men and business, far removed from the life of domesticity – were devalued. She managed that just by being who she was.

'Are you sure you won't be coming back with us for some morning coffee?' she said without actually looking at me. 'Sarah is abandoning us for an appointment with the carpet man. Can you believe it?' she continued, turning to Hugh. I noticed that she made no effort to include John in the invitation. The barefaced cheek of it annoyed me. How could she manage to be so rude to someone who had done her no harm, and was working so hard for the cause that she and Hugh believed in?

Then, as I watched the small twitch at the edge of his mouth and saw the amused glint in his eye, I realised that John saw Lucinda's snobbishness for what it was – and he did not give one damn. He knew his own worth and was not a man to be measured or derided by anyone. Her silly ways did not affect him one bit, unlike the rest of the village, who were overawed by her fine pedigree.

Something in me recognised a twin soul, and I think that is when I started to fall in love with him. He was right to feel sure of himself and to give respect only when it was earned, not because of birthright. It was the first, but not the last, important life lesson I learnt from him.

'I really must be going,' I said, briskly, wanting to get away before my annoyance showed. 'Thank you for the offer of coffee, but I'll be on my way.'

'I'm off too. Can I give you a lift?' John offered.

'I'd be only too glad of a lift,' I said. 'I really will be late, and I don't want to keep anyone waiting, especially as he has come all the way out from Armagh.'

Lucinda said nothing, but her smile and the little shrug of her shoulders told me what she thought of my concerns.

'My car is over here, Mrs Grey. We will speak again in the week, sir. Goodbye, ma'am,' John said, and we moved off together towards the car.

I didn't say much as I settled into the front seat. He looked straight ahead as he drove over the ruts in the lane leading back to the main drive. As we turned right, we picked up speed and he said,

'It looks like it will be an exceptionally good camp at Lindara. The two of them have really thrown themselves into making it go to plan. We need more like them to make the movement work.'

'You're all very committed to this, aren't you? I mean, I hardly see Theo these days, with all the meetings and the travelling he's doing.'

'Your husband is central to the whole thing, Mrs Grey. It is not at all easy to find a man who is trusted so widely. He has a particularly important job to do, handling the finances for the movement, and we are lucky to have the likes of him.'

'Theo is a perfectionist and, as you say, he's one of the few people everybody trusts.' I turned to him and added, 'But you're doing an important job as well, running about all over the Continent getting guns. It can't be easy for you.'

'Strictly speaking, you're not supposed to know what I'm up to.' He laughed and gave me a cheeky grin. 'Do you know something?' he continued. 'I love it. The travelling and the meetings and the talks into the night in smoked-filled rooms – I love every minute of it. It's not work to me. It's a real pleasure to be doing what I'm doing.' I could see that he meant every word of it.

'Well, it seems to me that they were lucky to have found you. You and Theo, Craig, Carson, Lord Clanhugh and all the rest – you make a fine team.' I realised as I said it that I meant it. While I had tried to stay on the sidelines and not get involved, I couldn't help but be impressed by the commitment and the drive of the group of men who were determined to have their way against all the odds.

'Oh, we need the young ones like Hugh and his lady as well. They are the ground troops who will make things work if it comes to the crunch,' he said.

'Lucinda is certainly throwing herself into it with great enthusiasm,' I commented rather dryly.

'She's a bit grand for the west of Ulster, some might say,' he said slowly, casting me a sidelong glance.

I hesitated because, while the sight of them together working as a team – and the perfect picture Lucinda presented – was meant to please and impress, all it had done was rake out the black kernel of hatred that I had felt for her from the beginning. I chose my words carefully, to ensure that John Brown would have no insight into my feelings.

'Oh, she means well,' I replied, 'but she hasn't got much sense when it comes to money. She has been used to having what she wants, I suspect, without the need to count the cost.'

'Well, it must be her who has the money, because it's not the Clanhughs,' he said.

His comment was unexpected, and I hesitated for a moment to consider the implication of what he said. Surely there was no problem with money for the Clanhughs? They had never given even the slightest inkling that they had any financial problems. They lived a stylish life, which was normal for people of their standing, but nothing about it, or them, struck me as extravagant or beyond what you would expect.

'What makes you say that?' I asked, surprised. 'Surely the Clanhughs have plenty of money?'

He hesitated and concentrated on manoeuvring the car through the narrow gates onto the road.

'Aye, you're right. They have all the money in the world,' he said finally.

I let the matter lie, as he was obviously reluctant to comment further.

In a few minutes we had reached the front of the hotel, and John pulled the car over to let me out. I thanked him and went inside, and I can't say my mind rested on the matter because I went immediately into the meeting. I thought no more about the Clanhughs or any money problems they may have had, but the information was tucked away in the back of my brain where it lay dormant, ready one day to come back and haunt my thoughts.

Chapter 11

THE TRYST

That autumn we were all on the go, full time. Theo was busy running the mill and fundraising, Hannah had her first child, which kept her and Mother fully occupied, and I threw myself into the management of the hotel. Samuel had adamantly refused to go back to boarding school in September, convinced that he would miss all the action if he did, so we let him enrol at day school in Armagh.

Hugh and Lucinda ran the camps, which were a great success, and the village was full of strangers while they were taking place. Some of the men arrived by rail at the nearest town and walked the last three miles, while others travelled from the local farms in pony traps. The village street was full at the weekends, as one set of trainees left and the next group arrived, and the hotel bar did a roaring trade. With that and the contract for supplying provisions, my side of the business was thriving.

While the Protestants had formed their militia, there were rumblings in Dublin and squabbling about whether they should do the same. Redmond resisted any call for a volunteer force, arguing that parliamentary means would deliver home rule to the Irish people, but there were those who did not agree with him.

In the autumn of 1913 the Irish Citizens Army was formed. This was mainly a talking shop for men armed with hurling sticks, but it caught the imagination of the nationalist-minded Catholics in the North. There were rumours that the O'Connell men were actively involved in the battalions that were being talked about, and I realised why Theo had been wary of them.

At that point, my life was settled and content. Even though we were in the midst of political turmoil, I blocked out the things I could not change and put all my energy into work. I did not dwell on the future and I assumed this was how I would live for the rest of my life. Because of the local politics in Ireland, I paid little attention to the rumblings in Europe – the tensions that would lead to war and to the devastation of many communities, even those as far from the fields of France and Belgium as Lindara. But the biggest upheaval of all for me was just about to happen.

As the hotel expanded, so did our need for space. I took over one of the stables in the yard and had it thoroughly cleaned, the walls whitewashed, and a stove installed in the corner. I furnished it with a desk, a chair and a cabinet with drawers for my work records. Then, to make it cosy, I added a carpet, a chaise longue, an easy chair and some bookshelves. I often worked there in the evenings, especially in wintertime. It was a bit of a joke with Theo, but I ignored him because I needed my own space.

As I sat there one evening the door opened with a soft clunk. A spear of light shot across the flagstones and then vanished quickly as the door closed. I turned from my desk, where my accounting books and papers lay in the sepia light of an oil lamp. The rest of the room was in shadow.

'Is that you, Theo?' I asked, as he stood still and silent by the door. Theo was the only person who ever ventured into my office in the yard, apart from the maids when they brought my tea.

There was silence and then a voice said,

'Sarah.'

I rose from my seat and stood for a moment in the heavy shadow.

'John? Is that you? What do you want?' I asked, softly. I did not need to ask. It is the kind of question that springs to your lips when you have nothing else to say.

How do you know when an affair begins? Is it when eyes meet and linger longer than necessary? Is it the covert smile across a crowded room, the look of joy when the admirer appears unexpectedly, or the hand lingering on the arm for those few seconds too long? Or is it all those things, leading to the inevitable?

I had known this moment would come, yet there had never been any conscious decision on my part about what I would do. There was no clear, fast marker of when a decision was reached. Rather, I had fallen into the knowledge of what would happen slowly and inevitably, like falling into a soft feather bed that encompasses you and will not let you go. I knew, you see, that the threads of our lives had already twisted together, even though we had never said anything of the attraction we felt for each other in the months of our acquaintance.

John stepped towards me. He took my hand gently in his, raised it to his lips and kissed it. I could see the outline of his face in the light. It struck me how young and fresh it was compared to Theo's ageing, grey complexion. I could see clearly the shadow of the hair growth on his chin and I thought of Theo's grey stubble in the morning when he woke, and the bush of grey hairs that sprouted from his ear as he lay on the pillow close to my waking line of vision. I breathed in John's distinct masculine smell. The aroma of smoke from the Havana cigars he favoured hung faintly on his coat.

He stepped closer and pulled me gently to him. His hands were soft on mine, for John had never done a hard day's labour in his life. He held me close and, while I did not go readily into his arms, I did not resist. He bent down and kissed me softly on the lips. I tasted the sweet, peaty flavour of the malt whisky he had been drinking. His kiss was long and deep and sensuous, unlike the dry closed-lip pecks that I had from Theo, and the desire for him surged in me. Then slowly my arms went around his neck and I kissed him back.

The room, and the accounts I'd been working on, and the business problems I had been mulling over, all faded from my mind. I was full of the taste and the touch and the scent of him. I was in his arms, aware only of him holding me, kissing me, touching me and taking me where Theo never could, and I was lost in him. By then there was no going back. We acted only by instinct that night, and it felt the most natural, beautiful thing.

I remember coming to my senses and fussing nervously, straightening my clothes and my hair. John smiled at me and then kissed me once more. I could read the look in his eyes and I knew that he was captivated, just as I was. He held me close and then said, with regret, that he had to go. I held him to me, for I knew he did not want to go, but the risk of being found in my private office was great for both of us.

He whispered that he would see me again as soon as possible. And then he was gone, striding through the door, across the yard and into the night.

When he was gone, I stood in a trance with no sense of time or place. In my mind's eye I went over every moment we had been together, each touch and kiss. I relived every minute detail. I sat down on the chair in a daze and thought how strange it was that this momentous thing had happened in such a seemingly casual way, with so few words spoken between us. It seemed crazy that I had allowed a man, someone not much closer than a stranger, to make love to me – and in my office, where we could so easily have been discovered.

Yet, it was as if I had had no choice. An obsession, for you could only call it that, had taken control of me. And even now, after the event, I did not feel any guilt about what I had done, even though I was an adulterous wife cheating on a husband who'd shown me nothing but kindness.

I knew already that this would be just the beginning for John and me. I sat there imagining our next meeting and where we might go and how we could arrange to be together and what we would do, without the slightest jolt of conscience. I needed more than the quick, furtive meeting that had just taken place. It was as if I had just discovered the passionate side to myself, even though I had been married to Theo for the best part of three years.

Theo's half-hearted fumbling had never aroused me the way that John had, but I also promised myself I would never be unkind to Theo – we were business partners and friends as much as man and wife.

But who could blame me for getting involved with John when Theo had his business and his politics, and had little real time for me? I had realised by then that my wooing and seduction of Theo had not been one-way. He had selected me carefully as his wife because I was precisely what he needed to run the hotel and let him get on with his political organising. Oh, yes, I had indeed been carefully chosen, although I did not know it at the time.

I was clear that John and I must not meet in Lindara again. It was too risky. We would have to arrange to meet in Belfast, or maybe even Dublin, when we were both away on business. I knew that if I chose this road, it would not be an easy one. However, I could not have guessed how, in between the excitement of the secret assignations and the stolen hours, days and nights together, I would have to live with the ache of waiting – never knowing when he would be in Lindara, and always aware that he was on the edge of danger and that I would, perhaps, never see him again.

Yet it was not in my nature to turn back. I had to take the risk and taste the experience because, for me, a life without risk was a life only half-lived.

Chapter 12

THE SPA HOTEL

To say that we were infatuated with each other would be an understatement. During the early months of 1914, I could think of no one else but John. He was in my thoughts every waking minute of the day. I went about my business as usual, but I had a smile in my heart at the thought of him. We were like a couple of teenagers in love for the first time.

I believed that what passed between us was for us alone and that, since it remained our secret, it could not affect those around us. When he came to Lindara I wanted to see him, yet I was always worried that we would give ourselves away. We could not keep from smiling in each other's company – we had to be careful to say a casual hello and then virtually ignore each other, for fear somebody would catch on.

I found plenty of reasons to go to Belfast on business, but even then I had to be careful. Theo was off about the province and, because of the secret nature of his business, I never quite knew where he would be. When John and I met in Dublin things were easier because we could be sure we would not bump into Theo there, but we still had to be constantly on our guard.

It was early in 1914 that we found the Spa Hotel. It was about twenty miles south of Belfast in the hilly drumlin country of County Down, within a short distance of the Mourne

Mountains, and we stayed there often as Mr and Mrs Brown. John was never short of money, and I knew that I could have anything I wanted when I was with him. This was before he made real money with the deals that were being set up in Europe but, even then, he had more than I was used to.

Never having to worry about counting the cost, we would treat ourselves to the best of everything. John knew of my love of fashion. He found an excellent ladies' outfitter in the local town and, happy to indulge me, took me there on a buying spree. It was bliss for me to be so pampered for the first time in my life, and, I admit it, I found it an easy role to assume.

We spent a long weekend there in late March 1914. The spring weather was glorious, and we took long walks in the surrounding countryside. It was a delightful time of year. Daffodils and primroses lined the banks of the country lanes, and the hillsides were bright yellow with gorse in bloom. There were plenty of walks that took us along lanes, round the lakes and past the neat little farms that dotted the countryside. All the while the peaks of the mountains lay in the distance. We used to go into the maze that was beside the hotel and play hide-and-seek in its deep green depths. Looking back, it seemed as if we laughed like children, happy and innocent.

The Spa was a small hamlet consisting of the hotel, a church, a school and a few houses. It was where some of the wealthiest local people had their homes. Many of the houses were large, built in different European styles, and set out in spacious, well-kept grounds.

'It would be nice to own one of these,' I used to say, dreaming of the day we would set up home together.

'I have my heart set on only one house. I'll buy it when I

have the money, and that won't be long,' he said.

'So, which one have you got your eyes on?' I asked.

He laughed and smiled down at me.

'Oh, it's not one of these. It's the house I've set my heart on this many a long year, and it'll be mine eventually.' He hesitated and then added, 'One day, Sarah, Carrick House will belong to me,' and put a protective arm around me as we walked.

He went on to tell me about his family and his childhood, and all the things that had made him the man he was. John's family had farmed land at Carrick for generations, and they had prospered with the growth of the linen trade at Lurgan. His grandfather had built the house for his family and reared two sons there: Roderick, and Walton, John's father.

John's grandmother was frail by nature but loved painting, and she had a special talent for watercolour landscapes. She'd always wanted space of her own to paint in and so, to please her, John's grandfather had built a folly in the garden. It had a curved staircase up to a first-floor room, which looked out on the wide vistas of the surrounding landscape. This was where John's grandmother used to go to paint, and to escape the raging arguments between her two sons.

According to John, Roderick and Walton never got on, even as children, and in later years they could barely stay in the same house without having a row. Roderick had his head in the clouds with poetry and music, and went off to study at Trinity College in Dublin where he got in with a crowd of rich and irresponsible young bloods. He was totally overawed by the social life and the culture of the place. John's grandfather always said it spoilt him, for he looked down on his own family after his time in Dublin.

Walton was the practical one, who loved farming and, in contrast to Roderick, never wanted to be anywhere but Carrick. When John's grandfather died, Roderick inherited Carrick House, along with the garden, the orchards and a few acres, while Walton was left the bulk of the farmland and a small cottage.

Within months Roderick sold his inheritance without a word to Walton. He did not tell him of his plans and never gave him a chance to buy the house. Walton always said that he did it out of spite. He bought a big country house south of Dublin and never came back north again. Walton always vowed he would get Carrick House back, but he never did. He farmed the land, brought up his three children – John, Fergus and Ginny – and stared at the house from afar, always dreaming that it would be his again.

But it never was. The family who'd bought it from Roderick had settled there and had no wish to sell so, even when Walton had raised the money for it, it wasn't on the market to be bought.

It seemed that every generation of the Brown family produced one son who was tied to farming as a way of life, and one that had no interest in it. In John's generation it was Fergus who was the farmer. He worked with his father on the land and took over the farm when he died.

Ginny, John's sister, had no love of farming. She hated getting her hands dirty, but she had inherited an artistic streak from the female side of the family. When she was a young lass she got herself a job with a hatmaker in Portadown, as much to escape the drudgery of the farm as anything. Her artistic nature blossomed from the start, and in no time, she was designing hats that were sought by all the ladies in Lurgan and Portadown.

Her boss saw her potential, and she was promoted steadily until she was running the whole design side of the business. She would go with him and his wife to London to all the great fashion houses, to see the latest styles, choose materials and get new ideas. Her reputation grew, and ladies from all the best families vied with each other for one of her creations. I knew of the hatmaker's reputation, but I had not realised that it was John's sister who was the designer.

John had never intended to farm. He always knew that was not the life for him. He had taken an apprenticeship in a grocer's shop to please his mother, but he knew that he would not stick with that. Even as a young lad he had plans for greater things, and then the opportunity of the gun business came his way and he grabbed it. From then on, he knew he had found the way to make his fortune. John was determined that, for him, the ambition to own the old family house would be more than a dream. I knew from what he said, and the set of his mind, that if he was determined to have Carrick House then no one in the world would stop him. I also knew that, with his taste for fine things, it would be a grand house, the best that money could buy.

As our last day at the Spa dawned, I felt tension building up in John. I ignored it at first, and then I tried to jolly him along with teasing and joking. All the time he played along, but as the day went on I could see he was more and more removed from me. I knew then that he was getting himself ready for something important. Finally, in the middle of the afternoon, I confronted him.

'What's bothering you?' I asked.

'Nothing. I'm fine.'

'I know there's something bothering you,' I said, gently. 'Don't take me for a fool, John. I'm not daft.'

'I have been thinking about the news from the Curragh. It's the main army base in Ireland, and it has been reported that the army officers there have refused to take up arms against the Ulster loyalists. Almost to a man they have said they will not fire on their own people, so it has put the British government into a tailspin.'

'But that is good news for you, is it not?' I asked, trying to get the information clear in my mind.

'Yes, it's very good news for us, as it strengthens our hand considerably.'

I still could not understand what was bothering him as the Curragh news was not something to worry about, but he did not say anything more. It seemed to me that there was something else on his mind, and I wondered how to get him to confide in me. We were halfway round Macauley's Lough and we sat down on the wall to watch the water rushing over the sluice gate. Two white swans glided past, dipping their orange beaks into the cold blue waters of the lough. A cool spring wind rippled across the surface and small waves broke rhythmically on the shore.

'I'm off to Germany tomorrow. It's highly secret and extremely important. I can't tell you any more than that, Sarah.' I watched the clouds drifting across the perfect blue of the sky and wondered if this would be our last day together.

'I know. I don't want you to tell me anything you shouldn't,' I reassured him, but I was quaking inside. I did not need to know the details of what he was involved in to know that, whatever he was doing, he would be in great danger. We sat together, our bodies touching, hand in hand, watching the reflections of the clouds drifting across the water of the lough, totally happy to be together.

'If all goes well and I do make it through this, I'll be rich enough to buy Carrick House. Then we will have a home of our own,' he said, smiling at me. I could see the doubt in his eyes, and he read the fear in mine. 'Don't worry. I'll be back,' he said firmly, holding me to him as if he would never let go.

I thought how incongruous the situation was, that I should be surrounded by people I loved dearly, who were all working for a cause that I did not agree with and would take no part in. While I did not agree with them and I would not help them, I still respected them and their rights to hold the views they did. It was a difficult balancing act, one which I succeeded in only because I flatly refused to discuss political matters. They had their views and I had mine, and we all had to live with that. It did not stop me worrying about them.

I was never concerned about Theo in the same way that I fretted about John. That was partly because he was involved with strategy and planning, and was rarely in the line of danger, while John was always under threat. It was also because I had already decided that John was my future, and that when all this trouble was over, it was him I wanted to spend my life with.

At that time, I never questioned whether he was driven by principle or by money. Nor did I doubt his loyalty to the cause. Yet only a few months later, guns were landed on a beach in the South of Ireland to be used by the Irish volunteers – and it was a Hamburg firm that had supplied both contending parties.

Chapter 13

GUNRUNNING

When I left John on that sunny spring morning in March 1914, I knew he was bound for Germany, but it was weeks before I heard the full story of what he'd got up to. I'm glad I didn't know much at the time, for I think I would have worried myself to death. As it was, I was on eggs for a couple of weeks as I knew he was in the thick of something.

John travelled by sea to Liverpool, by train to London and onwards to Dover. He then went by boat to Ostend and it was there that he met up with his two companions, men from the organisation who had travelled to Ostend separately, and together they took an overnight train to Hamburg. It was a long journey, but there was no fast and easy route to Germany in those days. His contact in Hamburg was a man called Bruno Kaiser, who was their main negotiator. Kaiser knew everybody there was to know in the arms trade throughout Europe, and in those days, Germany, Italy and Belgium were the main places of business.

John and his companions stayed in small hotels near the docks in Hamburg and kept in touch daily. When the final papers were signed and the deal was done, the three of them boarded lighters on the Kiel Canal, which were loaded with guns and ammunition bound for Ulster via the Baltic and the North Sea.

They spent the day going through the canal, and early the next morning they were on the open sea heading for the little island of Langeland, the closest Danish island. It was a sleepy place, nothing much more than a big bit of rock and sand in the cold blue Baltic Sea. There they rendezvoused with SS *Fanny*. The captain knew that he was expecting a highly secret cargo, and he had lookouts posted in the small town of Bagenkop to give warning of any unusual interest in the ship.

Over that weekend they transferred the cargo, some 216 tons of arms, from the lighters into SS *Fanny*. There were Mannlicher rifles from Austria, German Mausers, Italian Vetterli-Vitali rifles and five million rounds of ammunition. They worked solidly all day Sunday and into Monday morning, moving the cargo from the lighters that queued up nearby to unload. Then, once unloaded, they slipped away quietly back through the Kiel Canal into Germany.

They stopped for a bite to eat early in the afternoon of the Monday. As the final boxes of ammunition were being loaded from the last lighter, John heard the lookout's call.

'You'd better come up, sir,' one of the hands shouted down to the captain. 'There's a boat approaching.'

Everybody was instantly on guard. They were not expecting any boat. Indeed, they were not looking for any visitors at all. As they climbed on deck, John could see the gold trim on the coat and cap of the short fat figure at the front of the boat, and he knew at once it was customs. He glanced at the captain, who looked as unconcerned as you like.

'Leave this to me,' he said.

The captain, Sig, was a big, rangy Icelandic man – shaggy

and tough but with a cool, unflappable manner.

John and his two companions from Ireland could only watch and listen, although they could not understand a word. The captain was cooperative and helpful, as if he had nothing to hide. John watched the expression on the customs officer's face. He had a florid complexion, with protruding blue eyes and a pugnacious manner, and John's heart sank, for he knew that someone of his petty officiousness would insist on inspecting the cargo. They were incapable of doing anything as the officer and the captain disappeared into the hold.

John looked at the sea around the ship, wondering if there was any escape route open for them. He knew he would last no time in the icy cold of the sea, but there seemed to be no other way out. All he could do was walk the deck, smoke a cigar and wait.

An age passed. The boat rocked heavily on the waves that were being whipped up by an approaching gale. The crew of *Fanny*, the last remaining lighter, and the customs boat, sat and waited until finally the two men reappeared on deck. The atmosphere between them was formal and cold. The customs man spoke in clipped, authoritative tones, as if issuing a final warning, and then climbed back onto his boat and headed for shore.

'What happened?' John asked Sig.

'They seized the ship's papers. Put us under arrest, in effect,' he replied.

John watched him closely and he could see he was worried, but he was not a beaten man. Sig had something up his sleeve.

'He wasn't too sure of himself, our Mr Customs man. I leant on him just enough to let him know that he was out here on the high seas with only his shipmate for company.'

John smiled.

'You didn't threaten him, did you?'

'No, but all he could do in the circumstances was to take the ship's papers.'

Sig turned and smiled at John.

'As if I need papers.'

They watched until the customs boat disappeared around the end of Langeland and then Sig issued his orders. They were going to make a run for it.

They ducked and dived past ships and lighthouses as they weaved their way through the Danish islands that dotted the Baltic Sea. At times they ran with no lights on, for they knew they would now be regarded as most wanted. The Danish authorities were likely to think the guns were for the home rule movement in Iceland, which was a Danish protectorate, and would be very keen to intercept their ship.

When a storm blew up that first evening, though it made it heavy going through rough seas, it was a blessing, because it kept most of the Danish boats in harbour.

Finally, they were out of the Baltic and into the North Sea. They knew they were not in the clear, though. They still had to face the run through British territorial waters, where the British navy was on the lookout for them. There had been several seizures in recent months, all around the northern coast of Ireland, and the British were more vigilant than ever. John knew that every naval ship in the North Sea would be on the lookout for SS *Fanny*, so they were in effect sitting ducks.

The two other Irishmen were taken off at the Orkney Islands

and John was left aboard, the sole guardian of the cargo. News came through for them to hold up in the Scottish islands, well out of the way, and for days they steamed around, making little progress just to put in time.

John and Sig were sharing a bottle of whiskey over a game of cards when the orders came through. They were to head south immediately and meet SS *Clyde Valley* off the Tuskar Rock on the next night, 19 to 20 April. There they would transfer the guns. *Clyde Valley* would make the run into Larne, as SS *Fanny* had no chance of making it undetected.

'Great news,' John said, and laughed when he heard the arrangements. 'Somebody's kept their head about them.' He topped up the whiskey glasses and raised his to Sig's. 'Here's to your health, sir,' he said, as the glasses clinked together.

'We'd better turn in now. There's a lot of hard work to do tomorrow night.'

They sailed south at full speed overnight and kept near the coast during the day. When darkness came, they crept along with their lights out. Radio contact was restricted, so all eyes on board were looking out for the signal. They steamed slowly, keeping the noise of the engines low, with their eyes casting around in the gloom, trying to pick up the shape of a boat. They had strict instructions not to smoke on board, and by now the lookout crew were dying for a cigarette. The dark shape of the Tuskar Rock loomed up out of the darkness.

Then they saw it. A light beaming a distinct signal out into the night, flashing its vital message across the oily black of the sea. Sig was already turning to ease in beside the vessel, which was lying dark and silent in the lee of the Tuskar Rock. The engine was a low drone as the speed was reduced to a minimum. Slowly he manoeuvred, until they were right alongside the waiting vessel.

'Tie up at that end,' he called in a low whisper. The men knew what to do and the orders were minimal. In a short space of time, the two boats were lashed next to each other with nets tied between them and gangplanks in place. The holds were opened, and they began to lift the cargo out of *Fanny* and into *Clyde Valley*. The transfer of guns and ammunition took place with quiet efficiency.

They had been working for a few hours when John heard a noise.

'Listen. What's that?'

John thought he could hear a low throbbing over the steady hum of the crane and the shuffling of the boxes on deck. He listened again and then he was sure. He ran down the deck to Sig.

'I hear a ship, and it's a big one too. We need to stop all movement.' They listened. Already the sound was closer and clearer.

'Stop all movement,' Sig ordered in a low, urgent voice.

The order went around the ship. Within half a minute everything was still, and the lowlights that had been on in the holds were extinguished.

John and Sig walked to the stern of the boat to peer into the darkness. They could only see the black of the sea and the white tips of the waves breaking on the Tuskar Rock. They could hear the deep throb of large, powerful engines coming their way.

'Bloody battleship,' Sig said, as he cocked his head and listened carefully. 'It is, by God. A bloody battleship, no less.'

For the first time John heard anxiety in Sig's voice, and he realised that the ice-cool captain was a worried man. He was lashed to another ship and there was no way he could cut and run. He was trapped.

The ships lay together in the lee of the Tuskar without light or sound. It was as if the vessels themselves held their breath. In the distance, the nightlights of the battleship appeared and came steadily closer, heading straight for *Fanny* and *Clyde Valley*. There was nothing they could do. There was nowhere to go. With the gun power of a battleship closing in on them, they had no hope of escape.

The noise of the engine grew steadily louder as the ship's lights became clearly visible. They watched and waited. John felt a trickle of sweat down his back. He barely breathed as he watched the lights coming closer. Slowly the great bulk of the battleship bore down on them. Neither John nor Sig dared to speak.

Someone must have spotted them, maybe one of the local fishermen, and relayed details of the position to the nearest naval base. John thought of all the months of planning and the negotiations that had gone into this operation, the days and nights he had travelled all over Europe to set up the myriad deals that had led to the stockpile of guns lying in the hold underneath his feet. All the work and dedication that had gone into raising funds and planning. Now it was all lost.

Then John heard a low chuckle beside him. Sig said nothing. John felt irritated by Sig's sense of humour. Cool bugger that he was, this was no laughing matter. A few minutes later, he heard another low chuckle.

'What's up with you?' John whispered. Sig did not reply but John could sense him, like a predator stalking its prey, noting every movement of the progress of the battleship. As he turned to watch the ship too, *Fanny* rolled violently and John was thrown to the side. He banged his shoulder in the fall and got up with a groan. Sig was laughing now, a low nervous laugh.

'What is up with you?' John growled at him, rubbing his shoulder.

'The buggers are going past us, aren't they?' Sig said, pointing to the lights of the battleship. 'They're on their way into Lamlash. They weren't looking for us at all,' he said, laughing.

They had been so close to the battleship that they had been caught in its wake. It turned out that Winston Churchill had ordered it to return from Spain because of the emergency over SS *Fanny* and the rumours of gunrunning into Ulster. Sig had only been half right.

There were one or two minor casualties caused by the wake, which almost swamped the two ships tied together. With a great sigh of relief their work was resumed, and all the guns and ammunition were transferred.

The last transfer was John. He had to accompany the guns on the final, most dangerous leg of the journey, into Larne. As he said goodbye to the likeable rogue Sig, who was his kindred spirit, he gave him a handshake and a hug.

'Thanks for all you've done. If you need any guns for Iceland, you know where to come,' were his parting words.

Chapter 14

LARNE

Samuel huddled under the blankets in the front seat of the van and listened to the din of the rain blattering on the roof.

'When's it going to stop?' he asked.

'I don't think it will. It looks like it's on for the night,' I replied. Samuel wriggled his toes to warm them up and tucked his hands under his haunches. There was nothing we could do but wait. 'Shouldn't be too long now,' I said. 'We're about two miles from the first checkpoint and it'll only take us ten minutes or so to get there. We'll set off in about a quarter of an hour.'

Boyd, Theo's mechanic, was supposed to be driving that night, but his wife had appeared at the hotel in distress in the late afternoon. She said he was down at the pub, the worse for wear, and there was no chance of him driving to Belfast that night for Mr Grey. The poor woman was worried sick.

Boyd was the best of workers until he went on one of his binges, and then he was no good to man or beast. She worried about money and about him losing his job, and she had good reason to. Theo had been tempted more than once to fire him, but when it came to mill machinery and vehicles there wasn't the beat of him in County Armagh.

'Don't worry, Jean,' I reassured her. 'Theo's off in Belfast today, but I'll see to it. We just have to send somebody else.' Then, as she turned to go, I had a sudden thought and called after her. 'Jean, will you look at home and see if you can find the instructions he had from Theo, about where he had to be and when? Then bring them straight back here.'

Samuel was standing behind me in the kitchen and, when Jean had gone, I saw the look on his face and shook my head.

'No, Samuel,' I said. 'Don't even think of it.'

'Sarah, we can't let them down. This is too important,' he argued.

'I know that. I'm going to try and get somebody else to go.'

'There's nobody else Father would trust,' he said, and I knew he was right. This was a highly secret exercise, and Theo would trust no one but Boyd.

'You are not to do it. I have the keys of the van and I'm not giving them to you. You're not going, Samuel, and that's final.'

He started then, and brought up every argument he could as to why he should drive halfway across the province on this wet April night, because what was happening was so important that we could not let Theo down. I argued the bit out with him, but he wouldn't back down. He had the clear-sighted view of youth, that state of mind that only sees one solution. I was equally adamant that I could not get involved with anything political, having fought so hard with Theo and my family over the issues. It had been a long and weary battle for me to remain aloof from political action.

I don't know when I started to soften, but I finally realised that if I didn't let him go, he would find some way of getting to Larne that night. He was a sensible lad, but he was only fourteen and at times was capable of all the foolishness of youth.

I just couldn't allow him to go on his own. I couldn't let him take the risk. I knew I would never forgive myself if anything happened to him.

In half an hour we had the van prepared. We packed rugs and maps, food and drink, a tilly lamp and a spare bottle of methylated spirit. I got changed into thick dark clothes and put on an extra layer of underwear and socks, and by early evening we were ready. All we knew was that we were to be at the checkpoint outside Larne at one in the morning. We set off in great spirits, thinking of the time we had spent together learning to drive on the roads around Lindara.

We had been on the road since early evening in order to get to our destination well ahead of time. The journey had been easy at first. We came up through Armagh, Portadown and Lurgan, sticking to the main roads that were well sign-posted. After Lurgan we took the Belfast Road turning, just after Moira, to go north towards Antrim. It was after Crumlin that Samuel had to navigate, because by then we were cutting across country to Templepatrick and Ballyclare. We aimed to be near the first checkpoint shortly after midnight. It was always difficult to judge how long the journey would take, particularly in the dark and wet, so we had left plenty of time.

The going was quite slow on the small country roads, and I sat hunched over the steering wheel trying to see out through the sheeting rain. The eerie figures of trees with their bare winter branches loomed up in the dim headlights of the car. Every so often the road passed through the middle of a farm, the farmhouse twinkling its lights on one side and the dark farm buildings glowering on the other. The roads were muddy and spattered with cowclap near the roadside farms.

There was no one about to ask the way, even if we'd needed to, but we managed to get to the far side of Ballyclare by just after eleven o'clock. After a drink of tea and a bite to eat, Samuel settled down to get a bit of sleep. I could not fall asleep, even though I tried. My mind was too full of a mixture of excitement and the worry of it all – and I knew just what was at stake – while for Samuel, it was all just a bit of fun and adventure. As soon as he dozed off, my mind began going back over events.

Things had been progressing rapidly over the last three or four weeks. I knew something important was being planned but I did not know exactly what. One Monday evening at the end of March, Theo and I were eating a late supper when he was called to the telephone. When he came back, he had a face as long as a Lurgan spade and I knew that something was wrong.

'What is it?' I asked immediately.

'We're in trouble, all right,' he said, shaking his head.

'What do you mean? What's happened?' I asked.

Theo hesitated, choosing his words, because he knew that the information was strictly secret, but he did not believe in keeping me completely out of things. On more than one occasion I had been useful to him with advice.

'There's word through from Germany that the guns have been seized by Danish customs. Over two hundred tons of rifles from the Continent plus a million rounds of ammunition.'

'What were they doing in Denmark?' I asked, and then the story all came out.

'There's an awful lot of money at stake if this goes down,'

Theo said.

'Are any of our men with the cargo?' I asked, guessing at the identity of at least one of the people on board. Theo reeled off three names that I recognised, and John was one of them. I looked at his face, lined and grey with worry, and suddenly he looked every minute of his sixty-odd years. I realised just what a burden he was carrying by being at the centre of this whole affair and in control of large amounts of money.

'All we can do is wait and pray,' he said.

Neither of us slept that night. I could not bear to think of John languishing in some foreign jail for years and being unable to see him, yet I knew that was a strong possibility. What would I do if anything happened to him?

I got on with things as usual the next morning. On the surface of it I was my usual self, but inside I was frozen like a fly trapped in amber.

Then, at lunchtime the next day, the word we had been waiting for came through. SS *Fanny* had slipped anchor and made a run for the open sea in the middle of a gale. They were out of Danish territorial waters and presumed to be on their way back home. I couldn't help thinking that the Danes were probably only too glad to be rid of them, for it could have created a nasty international problem for the two countries.

The Times covered the story the next day, 1 April. The Danish authorities had thought the guns were for the subversives in Iceland, a Danish protectorate, but the paper told the world that the guns were bound for Ulster. Some people thought it was nothing but a crafty April Fool joke, which added to the general confusion. We were both delighted with the news, but we also knew we weren't out of the woods yet. The ship had slipped anchor and was on the high seas but there was no guarantee that she would make it to port safely. Even if she did the authorities were now aware, and would be on the lookout for her wherever she docked.

There was no more definite news of SS *Fanny*, and all we could do was wait. Time passed so slowly. Theo was on the phone on and off all day with other members of the business committee, and then by the evening he packed his bag so that he would be ready to leave at first light.

'I'm off to Scotland. I'll be away for about five days,' was all he said as he left. He was off to acquire a new vessel for the journey into Larne. They knew that SS *Fanny* would be stopped the minute she came into British waters, and so they urgently needed a new ship to transport the guns. Theo was on his way to charter SS *Clyde Valley*.

That same night, instructions were issued to the Motor Car Corps of the UVF. All available vehicles were to be outside Larne by midnight on the night of Friday 24 April. They were ordered to be punctual and ready for action for a very secret and important duty.

It was just by sheer fluke that Samuel and I had become involved. If Boyd had stayed sober instead of going on the binge, he would have been sitting here and not us. We had no way of knowing if the ship had managed to make it safely to Larne or if she had been stopped somewhere on the high seas. All we could do was follow the instructions and hope for the best.

'Wake up, Samuel,' I said, as I gently shook his shoulder.

It was getting towards midnight. 'Time to get moving now.' I stepped out of the van into the damp night breeze. The rain had stopped but everything around was dripping. 'Come and have a run up the road to warm yourself and get your circulation going,' I called.

'Not on your life. I'm staying here. I'll be all right,' he replied. I took a brisk walk up the road for half a mile and then ran back to the van once my eyes were used to the dark.

'Let's get moving,' I said to Samuel, lifting the starting handle to turn the engine. It turned over easily and we set off down the dark country road in search of the first checkpoint.

A dim light moved in a slow arc and loomed up out of the darkness ahead of us. It was indistinct at first, as a light mist had formed just above the surface of the road. We drew to a stop and two figures emerged out of the darkness.

'Good evening,' the voice said in the thick Scottish accent of the Antrim coast. 'Och here, it's a woman,' he gasped in surprise when he looked into the car. His big head disappeared out of the window and I heard him calling to a colleague that they had a woman driving this van and was it all right? I did not hear the reply but he must have been reassured, for he stuck his head back into the van.

He stared at me as if he had never seen a woman in his life before.

'Password, please?' he asked, while scrutinising me closely and then looking across at Samuel. I gave it. 'Right then, just head on down the road and you'll find the next checkpoint in a mile. They will direct you from there,' he said, and then tapped the roof of the van, giving us permission to go on.

The whole operation – codenamed 'Lion' – had been planned down to the smallest detail. Larne sat on the eastern coast of County Antrim and was the closest port to the Scottish mainland, which could be seen clearly in the distance. The local regiment of the UVF had taken over the port for what was claimed to be a test mobilisation, and Larne had been completely sealed off by late evening, with all routes into the town controlled. As we drove the last five miles the checkpoints came one after the other, and we became part of a stream of vehicles queuing up to get into the town. We could see the lights stretching ahead of us and behind us. In all some five hundred cars, vans and lorries had gathered that April night.

Each checkpoint was manned by three or four men, most of whom had already done a full day's work. They were all courteous and helpful, but careful nonetheless. At one or two of the key points there was spare petrol and a range of tools in case of breakdown. Thankfully, we didn't need them, but it was reassuring to know they were there.

By 2 a.m. we were moving steadily forward in a column towards the dock. As we rounded the last corner into the harbour, we saw the ship tied up. The name on her was clear: SS *Clyde Valley*.

'She's here,' Samuel exclaimed. 'They made it. Brilliant.' And he turned to me, his eyes shining brightly. Relief flooded through me. At least they had made it this far and John wasn't lying in a Danish jail.

I scanned the ship, looking at each of the figures on deck, in case I could catch sight of John. There were several men moving about but none that I recognised as him. I wondered if he had any idea that I was here, so close to him, but I knew

I would not be on his mind this night. He would not spare a thought for me, for he would be concentrating on getting the job done as smoothly and efficiently as possible. Theo was not on board. I knew he would be in some safe house near Belfast overseeing the operation and making sure it all ran smoothly.

Clyde Valley had two small local ships tied up alongside her. These were being loaded up, and were bound for Donaghadee and Bangor, just an hour's sail across the mouth of Belfast Lough on the coast of County Down. The ships were brightly lit, for there was no need to hide in the safe heartland of Ulster Protestantism. There were men everywhere, unloading and breaking down the cargo into piles, then moving the cars along the pier so that up to ten cars, vans and lorries could be loaded at the same time. Teams of people were loading the guns and ammunition into the waiting lines of vehicles. On the edge of the scene were the shadowy figures of the guards, guns cocked and eyes alert, ready to pick up the first signal that something was wrong.

The news had already come through that the authorities were swarming over another ship, which had been sent into Belfast docks as a decoy. The rumours about the *Balmerino* carrying guns had been carefully spread during the last week. The members of a UVF regiment in Belfast had marched to the docks to meet it, and they had been ordered to make as much nuisance of themselves as possible when the customs came to search the vessel. It was an essential part of the plan to keep the authorities well clear of Larne that night.

We drove slowly past the boxes piled high on the quayside, then moved forward and took our turn to have the van loaded with our consignment. Samuel jumped out and helped with the loading, while I stood to one side and watched. Everyone was in great form. These were men who had spent the day in the docks or in the fields of Antrim, yet they were working non-stop through the night to get the job done. There was a great sense of purpose and cooperation that night.

Then we had to start the long journey for home, back along country roads. I was on the edge of my nerves. I had a car full of guns that we had to get to the agreed dump outside Armagh by morning without coming across the authorities. It would be all too easy for something to go wrong, and as we drove those long dark miles I waited anxiously for the engine to splutter or for a tyre to go flat. At the slightest change of note of the engine I would stiffen and sit forward in my seat to listen, imagining the worst because I was so tense. We knew that *Balmerino* had been boarded in Belfast and we knew that it was only a matter of time before the authorities realised they had been bamboozled. There was every chance that, as we drove through the night laden down with the illegal guns, the news of *Clyde Valley* was spreading through the province and the police were being put on the alert for any vehicle that was on the move at this ungodly time of the morning.

Samuel sang like a thrush all the way home. I nagged at him that we were not home yet, but he would not listen to me. All he could say was,

'We've done it. We've done it.' We'd got the guns from under the nose of the authorities and we would deliver them to the farm outside Armagh, and of that he was absolutely sure. While I worried for both of us, he sang and navigated. The journey back often seems shorter, but that night it took forever.

We were just past the outskirts of Portadown when we saw the policeman. He was standing at the crossroads and it seemed he was watching for us. When he waved us over there was nothing I could do but pull in. There had always been the chance that, once the news was out, the police would have a province-wide lookout.

What could I say? I was busy trying to think of reasons for being out on the road in the middle of the night. We were coming home from a funeral in Belfast, I decided. Maybe that would get his sympathy. My eyes were already filling with tears as I got myself ready to act the part. If my story wasn't convincing and the policeman decided to search the van, then we would be heading for Crumlin Road jail.

'Oh, God-oh,' I heard Samuel whisper. 'What are we going to do now, Sarah?'

'Just stay calm,' I said. 'Let me do the talking.'

I stepped out of the van, trying not to tremble. I smiled a watery smile at him, wishing him good night. My heart was pounding, and all I could think of was the inside of the prison cell that was waiting for me. He looked slightly surprised when he saw it was a woman driving but he asked all the questions I had expected him to.

'Where are you coming from? Where are you going? Do you have any identification on you?'

I gave him the story about the funeral, stifled a sob and waited. He did not seem convinced. Then he asked for my name and address.

'You're Mr Grey's wife,' he said. 'Well, I thought it would be Boyd driving. I was just keeping an eye out to make sure everything was OK. On you go, and make sure you get back safely,' he added, giving me a big wink.

We didn't know that the telephone and telegraph wires had all been short-circuited between Larne and Belfast as early as nine o'clock the previous evening, as soon as the last train had gone down the line. Nor did we know that the lines to Bangor had been shorted at midnight, nor that the main line between Hollywood Barracks and the exchange had been taped and all conversations recorded. The planning of the whole operation was as near perfect as it could be.

The first streaks of dawn were stretching across the sky when we turned into the lane of Blaney's farm outside Armagh. There were a few hens scratching in the dirt as we pulled up outside the house. The front door opened, and a big red-faced man came out. He looked into the van and I could see the surprise on his face when he saw me.

'Where's Boyd?' he asked.

'He wasn't able to make it. We're standing in for him.'

'Oh, aye. On the bottle again?'

I did not reply, but I could see by the look on his face that there was no point in lying to him.

'Pull over to the barn thonder,' he directed. I reversed across to the barn, where his two sons appeared and unloaded the van for us in minutes. Even before we drove off, they had covered the rifles with bales of hay and everything looked the same as it had done less than half an hour before.

'Best be on your way, ma'am. You'll need your sleep. God bless you.'

On the last ten miles to Lindara I outsang Samuel from

happiness. The clouds had cleared and the morning sky was a pristine blue. The sun was up and doing a grand job of drying out the roads and fields after the drenching they'd had the night before. Primroses clung to the banks of the lanes in clumps, like great yellow cats' paws, and the song of the spring birds rang clearly through the crisp morning air. I drove the last few miles slowly, savouring the moment, even though we were both tired and ready for our beds.

I was so euphoric that the run was over, and we were home safely, that I did not stop to think where the night's expedition had taken me. It hadn't just taken me to Larne and back. It had taken me out of my position of neutrality and into the territory of an activist. I had been pulled into it because all the people I loved were involved and, when they needed me, my loyalty to them was more important than my own principles.

I'd done it for John and Samuel, and even a little bit for Theo, but in doing so I had betrayed a little bit of myself.

Chapter 15

WAR BREAKS OUT

After all the excitement of that April night and getting the UVF armed, the threat of war in Europe loomed. We all knew that if war broke out, it would take precedence over the politics of Ireland. There was still training and action in the summer of 1914, but our eyes were on the Continent and the troubles that were brewing there. I was determined, after that night of gunrunning, that I would not allow myself to be sucked into helping again, no matter what. I needed very badly to maintain my independence and stand by my principles for my own peace of mind.

Soon after that summer, Theo started his slow decline, after all action on the home rule front had ceased. By that October many of the young men from the movement had gone off to fight in Europe. It was as if the drive and the demand of the organisation had kept his mind in one piece, and when the pressure was off he started to disintegrate.

How can we judge when senility starts? You look back, but there is not a day or a week or month when you can say,

'That's when it all started, that's when he lost his mind.' You pick it up in the small things first, and with Theo it was his deafness and his habit of saying,

'Uh?' after everything, even when he had heard what you

said. If I did not repeat myself, he would answer my query after a moment or two when it had had time to sink in. Then he became very forgetful and was constantly losing everyday things like his keys or his pipe. We would have to hunt for them, and we would find them in the most unlikely places. Theo must have put them there, but he had no memory of it and denied any knowledge of it.

Later he got to the stage where he was deliberately hiding things, especially money or anything he felt protective of. He gradually became more forgetful and confused and he would wander into the kitchen and say to me,

'Where is Eliza?' The first few times this happened, I tried to explain to him that his first wife was dead and gone many years now, but he would have none of it. 'She must be about here somewhere,' he persisted.

I realised soon that the best way of dealing with this was just to say,

'Oh, she's just gone down to the shop,' or, 'She's gone down the road for something. She won't be long.' That was enough to keep him happy and prevent him from worrying. It was a simple game we all learnt to play for him. He could remember details and people and events from years ago, particularly his childhood, but he was unable to recall what he had done the day before.

Soon he started wandering off quite regularly. Some of the townspeople or a local farmer would find him two or three miles out of town, going nowhere in particular. They all knew him, and they would persuade him to turn around and walk with them, or get into a trap or cart and take a ride back to Lindara. He was generally benign at that stage and he would go quite readily, with little persuasion. I had to take on extra help because I worried that he would wander away after dark, or that he would fall on the road or in the woods and no one would find him. Over time he became more cussed, and then even violent at times. On more than one occasion I suffered a black eye or a swollen jaw when he took a swing at me, but I knew that it was all part of his illness and this was no more the old, mild-mannered Theo than I was the Jersey Lily.

It had taken me a time to realise that he was on a long, slow decline into senility. When I married him, I knew that we could not have a long marriage ahead of us. It was something I expected, but you do not dwell on death at that age or think of the many forms it can take. You expect death to come suddenly and cleanly in a decisive illness or an accident, a once-and-for-all event. You do not think that death can be a process over years in the form of senility. When you are young, you do not think of the consequences of having to live with the long, slow slide into death.

I don't recall when he started referring to the settlement, but it became a constant worry to him, one which he would fret over and badger me about until I was cross with him.

'There's going to have to be a settlement,' he would whisper to me.

'Of course there will, Theo. There will be a settlement in good time. Don't let it worry you,' I would reply in a confident manner. I had no idea what the settlement was, but it was best just to reassure him and keep his mind as much at peace as possible. It was a constant theme of his at that time and it was always said in a conspiratorial way, in whispers or when he pulled me to one side, out of hearing of the others.

Even when we were alone together, he would wring his hands and move nervously from one foot to another before he approached me and then, leaning to speak in my ear, he would say yet again,

'The settlement will have to be seen to, Sarah.'

At first, I thought that he meant the political settlement of Ireland, which had, in effect, been shelved while the country was at war. It had been readily agreed that the Ulster Volunteer Force should swing behind the British army in the fight against Germany, and many of the young men who trained in the Ulster camps of the summer and autumn of 1913 joined up at the first call to arms. In August 1914, there was a similar response from the Irish volunteers, and the two sides came together to fight the common enemy with very little discussion or dispute. The final decision on what would happen to home rule for Ireland had been suspended for the duration of the war, with the promise of a speedy decision once it was over. I assumed that this was what was on Theo's mind.

'It's all right, Theo. There will be a full agreement on the home rule question in time,' I said to him on numerous occasions, thinking this would satisfy him.

He would look at me and shake his head.

'Yes, Sarah, but there will have to be a settlement,' he would say, and I gave up in exasperation.

Over the next years he constantly returned to the theme and, though there were many times when months would pass without reference to the mysterious settlement, it always resurfaced and then he pestered me. In the spring of 1916, he became agitated once again and it was constantly on his mind. I thought at first he was upset by the news from Dublin where the Easter Rising had taken place, followed soon after by the execution of the leaders. Then it occurred to me that maybe he was more aware of events than we gave him credit for, and that perhaps he was concerned about the outcome of the war with Germany.

The events of the summer of 1916 were tragic for the whole of Britain, but no place more so than Ulster. In late June and early July, the men of the Ulster Division were fighting their hearts out at the Battle of the Somme. As dawn broke on 1 July in Ulster, the start of the marching season and the annual holidays, the most expensive day of the war was unfolding on the battlefields of the Somme. Of all the divisions taking part, the Ulster Division ranked fourth in the table of losses. The records show that they had over 5,000 casualties, 2,000 of whom died. By mid December, when the Somme campaign ended, Britain had suffered more than 400,000 casualties of war.

Theo must have had some kind of consciousness of the tragedy that was unfolding that summer, for there was hardly a family in the village not involved. The buff-coloured envelopes began arriving at doors throughout the area.

One of the first families affected was the Murrays, one of the biggest families in the village. Every one of them was part of our workforce at the mill. All the young fellows of fighting age in the family had gone off to war. The postman, Robert, looked pale and weary as he went on his rounds with the envelopes that almost always signalled bad news. As he got to a house where they had sons on the battlefield, the neighbours would crowd round the door waiting to hear the news and to be of help if it was bad, but there was no comfort for fathers and mothers who had lost their sons.

The morning Robert brought the news to the Murrays, he could barely drag himself up the street. He stopped at the hotel with our post and Theo was in the front hall.

'Fine morning,' Theo said to greet him. Robert could hardly find the voice to reply. He looked over Theo's shoulder at me and all the sadness of the world was in his eyes.

'Bad news,' I said, a comment rather than a question.

'Och, it's the Murrays, Mrs Grey,' he said.

'One of the boys gone?' I asked gently. Robert could barely speak. His big bony body shook with emotion as he tried to stop the tears from running down his cheek. It took a moment before he could trust himself to speak.

'If it was only one it would be bad enough, but I have two letters for them this morning. I don't know how I'm going to give them to Mrs Murray.' He stood in the middle of the hallway, his eyes asking me for comfort, but I could not relieve his pain.

Then out of the blue Theo spoke, in one of his rare moments of lucidity.

'One today and one tomorrow,' he said at once, and Robert and I looked at each other and then back at Theo.

'You're right, sir.'

The Murrays were not the only ones to suffer. Almost every family in the town with sons or husbands on the Somme heard bad news. Good news was the loss of an arm or a leg. Reverend Lavery had the job of telling many of the women that their loved ones were not coming back, for he often received news of the death before the buff envelope arrived.

We were blessed in Lindara with Reverend Lavery, for there was never a kinder man looking after a congregation than him. Over the summer and autumn months of 1916 he was seen going about the countryside, often finding families working in the fields, to give them the bad news. Eyes would raise from tying the stooks of corn as he walked up the road, because they knew that a visit from the reverend meant only one thing. For many of the families it was a matter of hearing which one of their beloveds was gone.

The tragedy was born on the battlefields, but it was mourned in the fields of Ulster during that long, sad summer. Through it all, the harvest had to be brought in and the animals fed and looked after. There was no let-up for grief in the round of daily toil.

Then, in the autumn, the gravely wounded soldiers who could no longer fight were discharged and began to come home. They struggled into Lindara, and we could see that the damage to bodies and minds was horrendous. Those poor lost souls came back with missing limbs, but the saddest ones of all came back without their minds. The youngest Murray boy was one of those. He was the runt of the family and his brothers had told him the army would never take him, but he was determined to follow them to France. He survived, but with both mind and body damaged. We took him on at the hotel to do jobs in the yard, and somehow, he struck up a bond with Theo and became his minder.

'Are you all right, yourself?' he asked Theo constantly.

'Och, aye,' was all he got by way of reply from Theo.

I overheard the japes about how there was not one good brain between the pair of them, but I knew it was said with the backhanded affection of country folk. It was that same quirky sense of humour that got Murray his nickname, the Colonel, for he was bossy with anyone who came near Theo. The Colonel only ever called Theo 'the Boss', and the two of them became a fixture in Lindara.

At times I watched them through the raindrops on the kitchen window, out in the yard together in the middle of the winter, and my eyes would mist up, seeing these two injured men working together. I was relieved to have the Colonel's help because, even with the damage to his mind, he had a kind nature and a good heart. Theo touched some deep part of him and, as he came to realise that he was at home in Ireland, far from the horrors of the trenches, he slowly regained his sense of self. I did not know then that the Colonel would look out for me and my loved ones for years to come.

Theo still seemed to have some cognizance of the events so, when he mentioned the settlement, I referred to the war and tried to calm him by agreeing that there were indeed signs of a settlement.

'It will end very soon,' I told him, but it did not seem to satisfy him. 'But what settlement do you mean, Theo?' I would then ask. He would step back, look me in the eye as if I was being impertinent, and withdraw as if he had something to hide.

Everyone suffered in those hard years of the war, and even the Clanhughs were not immune. Hugh joined the army, as all his class did, at the first call to arms. The poorest in Ireland had always joined the British army as their way of getting a living, while the upper classes joined through a sense of duty to their country. Conscription was never imposed and many of the middle classes had to make their own choice. When he went off to war, Lucinda spent much of the time back in England with her family in Yorkshire. She never really settled in Ireland, and we always felt that the life here was not grand enough for her.

One morning in the winter of 1916, Lord Clanhugh died as he walked across to the home farm. He had a massive heart attack and he was gone instantly. Lady Clanhugh was devastated, as she had been utterly devoted to him. She seemed to die a little herself when he was gone, and though all her friends rallied round to help, she seemed to give up all interest in life after she was widowed.

The house was like an empty shell with Hugh on the battlefields of France and Lucinda in Yorkshire with her family. Lady Clanhugh struggled to keep things going, but it was hard for her as she had never had to manage anything more than the menus and the housekeeping. We all wondered when Hugh would come home to take charge of the estate, but the months went by and the news from the front was as bad as ever. There was no sign of him being released from duty. Lucinda managed to meet him briefly in England, but his leave was never long enough to allow him to travel to Ireland.

It was late in the autumn of the following year that Hugh was invalided out of the army, and returned home to the estate with Lucinda and their son. It was only then that I got an inkling about the issue of the settlement that had been torturing Theo's mind for so long. Hugh came back an older, greyer man with a stoop in his back and a serious limp. Like the rest of the returned servicemen, he had stories of horror but he was reluctant to dwell on them. We could see the anguish in his eyes, and those of us who had been lucky enough to stay at home did not want to punish him further by questioning him about the war or asking him to relive his nightmares.

Theo stopped dead in his tracks when he saw Hugh coming through the door of the hotel one morning, a week after his return. He recognised him immediately, which was unusual by this time. There were days when he was not even sure who I was.

'Hugh,' he exclaimed. 'Good to see you, boy. How are you?' And he shook him firmly by the hand.

'Theo … fine. Well, as fine as one could expect to be,' Hugh replied with a slight smile. I was busy mouthing over Theo's shoulder that he wasn't himself, but I could see that Hugh didn't understand.

'How are things?' Theo continued.

'As well as can be expected. Lucinda is fine and Maxwell is such a dear little boy.'

'How are things?' Theo repeated.

'Well, fine,' Hugh said, hesitantly.

He looked at Theo closely and then his gaze moved to me. He turned to me and bowed slightly as he took my hand.

'Sarah … good to see you.'

Then, as he leant towards me, he whispered,

'Is Theo all right?'

I stepped back from him and took in this frazzle of a man, who was two years older than me but who had a lifetime of horror etched in his eyes and on the lines of his face.

'Just ageing a bit,' I answered. 'Aren't you, dear?' I said, turning to Theo. I could see the light of understanding slowly come into Hugh's eyes.

Theo moved close to Hugh and leant to whisper in his ear.

'You will have come about the settlement, then.'

Immediately, I looked from one man to the other. Hugh stood still but I sensed the tension in him. It was as if he'd pulled himself into some central core so that he could keep himself fully and completely under control.

'What settlement, Theo? What do you mean?' he asked quietly. A small muscle throbbed in his cheek.

'Now that Clanhugh is dead and gone, you will have come about the settlement,' Theo whispered.

'I'm sorry, Theo. I'm not sure what you mean.'

'The settlement. We must sort out the settlement,' Theo whispered more urgently.

Hugh glanced at me for help and I shrugged slightly. I looked at the man in front of me and saw only the small boy with dark bright eyes, who could lie his way out of trouble with an audacity that had left me breathless as a child. I saw the young man who swore there would be no one else for him but me, only weeks before he returned to Lindara with Lucinda.

I looked at him as he confronted Theo, and I knew with certainty that he was lying.

He turned back to Theo.

'We'll see about the settlement, Theo,' he said, patting his arm as if to mollify him. 'We'll see about the settlement.'

And then he turned on his heel and went out through the front door of the hotel without saying another word.

Chapter 16

DUBLIN

Through all this, John and I continued to see each other whenever we could. We did have some rows and misunderstandings. Which lovers don't? Once in a while it was a more serious argument and we would not speak for weeks. I'd think to myself,

'Right, that's it. It's over,' but then he would contact me, and my resolve would melt, and I'd agree to meet him again. I suppose I was hooked on the thrill of it all and needed the excitement, as well as the love and affection. It gave me something to look forward to and it was a relief from the routine of looking after the business and Theo.

When the war broke out I wondered if John would volunteer, but he decided not to. He simply said that his business interests had grown and that there was no one to run his affairs if he went off to war. He said that he dealt in machinery, and that the business had grown naturally out of the contacts he had made during the gunrunning. He did not travel to Europe so much because of the war, but he was regularly in America and he spent a lot of time in Dublin and Cork. I accepted what he said and rarely questioned him. Why should I?

When change happens right in front of us, we do not see it until we are made to see it. The shift in others is often slow and gradual, and we are so involved in living our lives, in getting through each day, that we don't stop and take in the change of course in the minds of those around us. We are slow to notice the dropping in the jaw and the greying of the hair, the extra lines around the eyes or the extra inch around the waist. Then, one day we see those nearest to us with a stranger's eye, and we realise how much they have changed without us realising it. We see it even less in ourselves for, while we know each inch of the internal journey we move along, we rarely stop to look back across the landscape and see the distance we have travelled.

I sat in the foyer of the Shelbourne Hotel in Dublin one afternoon, taking tea and resting after a long day shopping. I loved visiting Dublin because my favourite shop imported clothes from Paris, Rome and New York. I always spent the morning checking out the styles they knew would appeal to me and receiving the best of personal attention. I was allowing myself a rare treat – a holiday from the constant struggle of looking after Theo, and the hotel, and overseeing the mill business.

Samuel was helping to run things now, and he proved to be a great asset. He and I worked together easily, with little friction. He was also great with Theo, taking him with him in the car when he went to collect things for the mill. He had grown into a considerate and thoughtful young man.

There was a lightness of mood in Dublin that wasn't to be found in Belfast, for although many men from Ireland were fighting in the fields of Flanders there was a sense that it was not their war. It was an English war, not an Irish war. The uprising at Easter in 1916 had been a disaster, with all the leaders caught and shot, and yet that very act had raised the awareness of nationhood beyond the hopes of the organisers.

As I drank my tea, I watched the hotel customers come and go. There were ladies in their finery, men in their business suits, a few American tourists, but nobody was in any rush to go anywhere.

Then three men caught my eye as they came down the long corridor to the foyer. One was tall with dark hair and a thick black moustache. He was definitely foreign, though of which nationality I was not sure. One was older with a bald head and a stout build, and he had the look of an Irish farmer about him even in his expensive city business suit. The third one was John. He had an air of authority about him, even at a distance. You could tell they were men of position and power. It dawned on me as I watched them that John fitted among them as naturally as a boulder of granite in the mountains of Mourne.

I watched as John and the younger one talked, finishing the details of a deal, while the older one listened closely. They stood to one side of the foyer, intent on their business and unaware of being watched.

It was then, seeing John with a stranger's eye, that I realised how far he had come. Only five or six years ago he had been an apprentice in a grocery shop in Armagh, serving his time with no higher goal in his future than the management of the shop when Mr Shaw retired. He had moved from that to running the gun club, then to buying a few guns, and on to organising the whole of the gun-buying programme for the movement. With each step he had grown in confidence and in stature, but I had not realised quite how much he had changed until that afternoon. Even then I did not know the half of it. I had no idea just how much wealth he had accumulated for himself in those few short years.

I turned slightly away from them, and I was glad that I was wearing a hat and that the wide brim hid my features. I lifted the silver tea strainer and set it carefully on the china cup. I poured a second cup of tea from the silver teapot, added a small quantity of milk to the cup, and then stirred it slowly, taking the chance to glance sideways at the three men from under the brim of my hat.

They were still in the same place on one side of the foyer, but their meeting had obviously come to an end because they were shaking hands and preparing to say their courteous goodbyes. Within a few minutes the foreign gentleman disappeared through the door, and John and the older man remained. They talked intently for a few minutes, their heads close together, then with a quick goodbye and a handshake the older man was gone. John turned and went directly upstairs to our room, completely unaware of my presence.

We lay in each other's arms that evening, and while John seemed relaxed and content I could not settle. My mind kept going over what I had seen that afternoon. I was cautious about tackling John on the subject, yet I knew that I had to if I was to put my mind to rest. There had been rumours. Snippets of gossip had reached me in Lindara that he was now supplying guns to the Republicans, but I had not paid attention to any of them. Now, since seeing John with those two men this afternoon, I had begun to run them through my mind again and wonder.

'Who was that man you were with today in the hotel?' I asked him.

'Which man?' he answered vaguely, although I could feel him tense beside me.

'As I came back this afternoon, I saw you saying goodbye to an older man.'

He paused for a moment.

'Well now, that must have been Seamus McGuire. I was doing a bit of business with him. Why do you ask?' he said, turning towards me.

'Oh, I just wondered,' I replied. 'I didn't know you had a meeting in the hotel. I thought you were going to an appointment over near the Four Courts.'

He paused.

'That was earlier. Then I came back here to meet Seamus.' He moved away from me slightly and was thoughtful for a moment. 'He's a very wealthy guy, Seamus, though you wouldn't know it by looking at him.'

'What does he do?' I asked, watching him carefully. John lay back on the pillow and laughed.

'What does Seamus do? Oh, this and that. Seamus is into anything and everything that will make him a pound or two,' he replied. Then he pulled me to him and kissed me. 'Let's not worry about Seamus. There are much more interesting things to think about.'

I kissed him gently and then pulled slowly away from him and got out of bed. I moved to the window and looked down over the gaslights glowing around the edge of St Stephen's Green. The street was full of cars and carriages, as it was still early evening.

I looked back at John stretched out in the bed patiently waiting for my return, and I thought how much I loved him, but how little I really knew about his life. I had no real idea of what he got up to, who he was with or how he made his money. He always seemed to answer me willingly when I questioned him, just as he had answered me readily about Seamus, adding little titbits of information about him, but not really telling me anything at all.

'What sort of business are you doing with Seamus, John?' I asked.

He looked at me in surprise.

'What brought this on?' he asked, teasingly. 'You don't want to bother yourself with my business. You're supposed to be having a break, not worrying about my business problems. You have enough of your own with Theo.' He smiled at me and stretched out a hand to me. 'Come here now and stop worrying yourself about business. It can wait until tomorrow. We have so little time together as it is. Come here.'

I turned instead to look out of the window, breathing in the scent of the French perfume John had bought me, which lingered on my negligee. I turned to face him. He lay on the bed raised up on one elbow watching me, waiting for me to come back to him. I loved his dark liquid eyes like the brown-green silky water in the marsh streams of Lindara, yet their softness belied the steel that lay behind them.

'There have been rumours, John.' He lay silently, not making any rush to answer me. 'I think you should know about them.'

I watched him, but his expression did not change.

'So, what have you been hearing about me, Sarah?'

'They say you are running guns for the Republicans now, the Sinn Feiners.'

'And who has been saying that?'

I pulled the curtain back and looked out again, part of me not wanting to pay heed to my suspicions, part of me needing to know more.

'Just some of the young lads talking. Samuel picks up their bits of gossip and brings them home.' I turned to look at him. 'You see, I couldn't help wondering when I saw you with those men today, because you hadn't mentioned a meeting at the hotel. You said you would be down near the Four Courts on business. So, when you hadn't said anything about them … well, you can imagine how my mind went racing trying to think what the explanation was.'

He lay there smiling and nodding his head.

'And then you put two and two together and made five, didn't you?' He smiled at me. I dropped my head to turn from his gaze. His ease about the whole thing made me feel stupid. 'Come here, Sarah,' he said, and put out his hand to me. I moved across and sat on the bed. 'No, come in beside me. I want you here with me.' He drew back the cover and pulled me into bed. He kissed me gently, but I was not to be sidetracked just yet.

'So, what was your meeting with the men about?' I persisted.

'It's all quite simple, you know. I made some incredibly good contacts when I was buying the guns for the UVF. Many of the companies I dealt with make machinery as well as armaments, and it is those connections that I am putting to use now. Ireland is developing fast, and the factories need machines. Even though Europe is at war, there are people doing ordinary jobs and making machinery. Seamus is a businessman who's into everything if it makes some money, and that's what I'm doing too. I'm using my connections, and I know how to buy and sell whatever people want.'

He turned to me.

'I don't blame you for worrying. It is only natural that you should have your doubts if you're hearing rumours about me. Just take it from me: I'm only interested in business and making money. Politics and freedom fighting are for other people, not for me.'

He kissed me then, and I lay feeling relaxed and at ease for the first time that evening. He had not evaded the questions, his answers were simple, and he hadn't tried to lie or cover up. I believed him because I wanted to. I was not ready to deal with any other truth.

Yet, a small part of me didn't accept his explanation. Before the spring of 1914, I had been happy to have John treat me and I'd enjoyed sharing with him the good things that his money could buy, but after that time I was careful to use my own money for my expenses. It was easy to justify because I needed receipts for the account books and I couldn't indulge in travel and have no expenses to show for it, but the real reason was that I wouldn't accept our meetings being paid for if it was with his dirty money.

It was hard enough to accept John trading in guns when I believed it was a matter of principle, but the thought of him becoming a mercenary was a step too far for me. I loved him as much as ever, and we were both still totally happy when we were together, but there was doubt in my mind about the source of his money and I was happier keeping my independence and paying my own way.

Chapter 17

MYSTERY TOUR

John arrived out of the blue one hot sunny Saturday in the summer of 1918. His visits to Lindara were sporadic, and we never knew when he was likely to show up, but that day I could see immediately that he had something up his sleeve.

He roared into the kitchen, greeting everyone with a hearty hello, grabbed Violet round the waist and stole a bun from her, punched Samuel on the arm in a jokey man-to-man gesture, and suddenly the whole place was alive and buzzing. Theo came into the kitchen and beamed at the sight of him.

'How are you doing, Theo?' John said, pumping his hand and smiling at him. 'And Sarah, how are you keeping?'

'Grand, John. How's yourself? Long time no see,' I added, with a touch of irony only he would have noticed. I hadn't heard from him for more than three weeks. Normally he kept me well informed about his whereabouts and I would know when he was due back.

'I have been terribly busy the last few weeks, but now I've got a wee surprise for you all.'

'What is it?' Samuel asked immediately.

'Well, it wouldn't be a surprise if I told you, now, would it?'

We all stopped what we were doing and looked at him, waiting to see what he was going to say, but he just laughed and said to Violet,

'Get a few of those buns and some lemonade into a basket for us. We're going on an outing.' Then he turned to me, 'That's all right, isn't it?'

I hesitated. My day was full of plans and I had plenty of work to fill it, but something in me caught his mood and I thought,

'Blow the work. Let's have a treat.' I smiled and answered,

'Yes, fine. Where are you taking us?' I added, though I wasn't quite sure who he intended to include in this outing.

'Another nosy one,' he joked. 'Didn't I say it wouldn't be a surprise if I told you? Well, Theo? Are you game?' Theo just stood there smiling and nodding. It was one of his better days, when he was gentle and easy to handle.

'Can I come too?' Samuel asked.

'You can indeed. You, Theo and Sarah – you're all my guests on a mystery tour,' he added grandly.

Violet bustled around getting food and drink into a picnic basket and I went upstairs to get changed into better clothes. I could hear them chattering in the backyard while they packed John's car with the picnic and a rug. I had no idea what he was up to as he had never surprised us in this way before, yet I could see by his high spirits that something was behind it.

We set off, Theo and I in the back of the car and Samuel in the front beside John. We took the Armagh road, but he wouldn't tell us where he was heading. It was hot, and clouds of dust blew up on the road behind the car. Samuel and John chatted easily in the front, while I sat quietly in the back with Theo. I was relieved to see John again and to know he was all right after his three weeks of silence. The notion of scolding him vanished now that he was here and I knew he was safe.

We didn't stop in Armagh but carried on straight through the city on the Portadown road. By then I really was wondering where we were going, but I had no idea what he had in mind for us. At Portadown, John turned right and headed south on the Guildford road and I got an inkling of what was to come.

'Has he finally managed it? Is this what it's all about?' I thought.

We turned left into a country lane and the car slowed down, taking the tight bends slowly, and negotiating round the deep ruts and potholes. We came to a crossroads where there was a small plain Presbyterian church and a few cottages, and I guessed that we were in Carrick.

'Just wait. We're not there yet,' he cautioned me as I made to question him. I had no choice but to sit back and wait. As he slowed, I saw a small cottage with a young woman sitting on the seat outside, sewing what looked like a large brimmed hat. She looked up at the sound of the engine and her face lit up with pleasure.

'John,' she said, 'what are you doing here?'

'Ginny, come and say hello.' She walked across the garden, her slim frame erect and elegant, smiling broadly at us. 'Ginny, meet Mr and Mrs Grey and their son Samuel. This is my sister, Ginny.' We exchanged greetings and I was very pleased to meet her, having heard so much about her.

'Where are you off to?' she asked.

John grinned and winked at her.

'It's a mystery tour. Do you want to come along?'

Her eyes danced with joy and she said,

'Indeed I do. Just hold on, and I'll wash my face and put on a clean blouse.'

'Not at all. There's no need for that. We're not going far,' John said. 'Just climb onto the running board and hold tight. I'll go slowly and you'll be safe enough.'

Up the road from the cottage we rounded a bend, and before us on the hill was a large Georgian house built in grey stone. It was a classic Irish country house, but larger than most and set in a fine position, with good views over the surrounding countryside. We drove up the narrow lane and stopped in front of the house.

'My new home,' John announced, and I smiled to see him so happy. 'Come and have a look around.'

We stepped out of the car and turned to take in the views. The countryside was perfect in its summer glory, and there was a real feeling of peace and tranquillity surrounding the house. But when I turned to look at the house up close, I could see that the windows were dirty, the paint was peeling, and it looked a lot less attractive than it had from a distance.

John opened the front door and we followed him inside. It was a great disappointment. The hallway and staircase were dark and dingy, and as we followed him from room to room an awkward silence grew as the four of us searched for words of approval that would sound sincere. John was so taken up with the place that he didn't seem to notice our reticence.

Finally, Samuel broke the silence and voiced what I was feeling but didn't dare say.

'It's a great house, John, but you are going to have to do an awful lot of work on it. It will need a lot of modernisation,' he ventured cautiously.

John laughed.

'You can say that again. I'll be spending a fortune on it before I'm finished, but then it will be just exactly as I want it.'

He started to talk enthusiastically about his plans for Carrick House and how he intended to put in running water, bathrooms, electric light, a new kitchen and all the latest equipment. He would then fill the place with the best of antiques. I listened to him and remembered how I had achieved so much at the Lindara Hotel, and suddenly I was swept along by his enthusiasm.

He turned to me and said,

'So what do you think, Sarah?' His eyes were bright with excitement like a child with a puppy.

'It's got potential. Most definitely it's got potential,' I said, after the slightest hesitation, aware suddenly of Ginny's eyes on me, watching carefully.

'That's what I like to hear. Someone who can see what can be done rather than seeing the problems,' and he smiled at me while I looked away, worried that his feelings were a bit too obvious.

'That's partly why I asked you here, Sarah. I know what a good job you've done with the hotel, and I was hoping you'd give me some help with this. It's going to be a big project, and you have such good taste and you know where the best suppliers are. So, what do you say? Will you give me a hand?'

'Of course, I will,' I agreed. 'I'll be more than happy to help.' It would give us the perfect excuse we needed to see each other, and I would thoroughly enjoy doing up Carrick House, particularly since we both knew it would be our home one day.

We looked around the rest of the house and then we went into the yard for a quick inspection.

'Are you going to farm the land?' Samuel asked.

'No. Farming isn't for me. I'm not here enough to farm, apart from anything else. My brother and his family will farm the land. They live at the cottage we passed at the end of the lane. He's been hoping I would manage to buy the place so that he could expand his holding. He has two growing sons and they both work for him, so they will be more than able to cope with the extra work.'

'Let's show them Grandmother's room,' Ginny said, and John and she turned to lead us round the side of the house through a walled garden.

At the end of the garden stood a stone tower. John lifted the latch on the old rotting wooden door. It had dropped on its hinges and it caught slightly on the stone step, making a sharp screech that set my teeth on edge. He pushed against it and it gave way, and in the gloom I could see the steps of a narrow staircase.

We went up the steps in single file, into the small first-floor room that had been his grandmother's studio. The view across the green summer countryside to the misty shadows of the distant mountains was glorious. We stood quietly, admiring the panorama, and I thought how privileged she was to have had this room with such a view. Would it be mine one day?

We went back to the car, lifted out the rug and a picnic basket, and carried them across to the front lawn. We spread everything out, and Ginny and I settled on the rug while the men sat on the grass to eat the picnic.

'You've had your heart set on this place for a long time,

haven't you?' I said to John.

He looked at me with a faraway look in his eyes as he said,

'I've wanted Carrick House since I was a nipper. It's always been a goal of mine to get it back, but it just took longer than I thought. The old fellow who bought it from Uncle Roderick died a few months ago and I had to negotiate with the family. He left it to his only son, who now lives in New Zealand, but he didn't want to keep it and that's how I got my chance.'

I smiled at him, glad to see him so happy.

'I'm so pleased for you, John. I'm sure you'll make it a beautiful home.' And then the devil in me couldn't help adding, 'All you need now is some good woman and a handful of children to fill it.'

'There's time enough for that. Sure, I'm only a young fellow yet. Too young to be tied. Isn't that right, Samuel?' John laughed and Samuel joined willingly in the joke, oblivious of the undercurrents between us.

I could see Ginny's eyes watching us, moving from me to John, listening to what we said and reading the unspoken language between us. I realised that we needed to be careful and I could tell that she suspected there was more than just friendship between us. And I wondered if she knew that Samuel and Theo were just there for cover.

It was as if a shadow fell on me as I sat there, and I cringed inside with embarrassment. It dawned on me that, although Ginny was being perfectly pleasant to me, she saw me as the scarlet woman, the seductress, who was a threat to her older brother even though he was a grown man and capable of looking after himself. Why had I not realised this before? Did I really think that because we'd been discreet and kept our affair secret that it wouldn't seep out into the rest of our lives?

I was suddenly overcome with guilt and a cold sweat broke on me, even though the day was warm. It was the first time I had stopped to think that what happened between John and me could have a bearing on everyone else, except Theo, of course. I had never taken John's family or their concerns for him into account. It just hadn't occurred to me to see it from their point of view, but now I slowly realised that life was never that simple.

I lay back on my elbows and watched as John and Samuel wrestled with each other on the grass like a pair of young cubs. They were both so vibrant and full of energy, while Theo sat on the grass eating his buns, content to let the world slide by. He got up then and wandered off, and I joined him, holding him by the arm and leading him round the garden, looking at the trees and the plants. He had never had time for things like gardens before – politics, fishing and business were his interests – yet he walked calmly with me and listened as I talked. I knew most of the plants by name, since my mother and father had both been keen gardeners.

I could hear the shouts and whoops of John and Samuel as they continued with their horseplay in the field in front of the house, but for the first time in years I was content with Theo, knowing that I was making the last years of his life as tolerable for him as possible.

'What is going on in your mind?' I often wondered. 'Does he know that he is gaga, that he doesn't make sense, and that at times he is an object of fun to the children of the village? Does he have any sense of who he has become?'

I was suddenly filled with tenderness for him. Here was a

man who had always been so clever, so confident, so decisive and respected, and now he was like a child. Samuel and I had to wash him, help him to dress and make sure he was watched over – and sometimes, now, hold on to him carefully as he walked with his stumbling gait. The tenderness I felt for Theo was followed by a sharp tinge of guilt as I thought of my secret plans with John. I knew then that for all my wishes and dreams I could never leave him, and I would stay with Theo until the day he died.

Chapter 18

VIOLET SUSPECTS

Violet's wise old eyes followed me round the kitchen as she spooned hot fat over the eggs sizzling in the pan. The smell of frying bacon filled the air.

'You're not looking yourself at all, Mrs Grey,' she said. 'Are you sure you're all right?' Violet did not miss a trick. She wasn't easy to fool, and I had more than enough reason to feel poorly.

'No, not great,' I admitted. 'I can't get a decent night's sleep with Theo at the moment. He is up and down half the night wandering about and chittering on at me all the time.'

'Och sure, you need a bit of help. You can't keep on like this.'

'I'm still tired from Christmas and the new year. I never got a minute's peace the whole time and I haven't stopped since.'

I watched as she deftly tipped the pan up and scooped the fat over the yolks to cook them to a perfect pale cloudy yellow.

'You should get Jean to come in at night sometimes and give you a break. She can handle him grand. He would listen to her and you'd get yourself a bit of peace,' she said, as she watched the eggs.

'I could do that,' I replied tentatively, and then I smelt the bacon fat and I felt the bile rise in my throat. I left the kitchen quickly before she could see how nauseous I felt.

I knew I was pregnant. To begin with my mind tried to deny what my body could not. When I first felt a touch of sickness, I immediately wondered what I had eaten to upset me. It could have been the pork we had the night before, I reasoned, and when I felt sick again, I thought perhaps I had picked up a stomach infection. But as time went by there was no getting away from it, and I eventually had to admit it to myself.

I wiped my face and hands and looked at myself in the mirror. My features did look thinner and there were shadows under my eyes. I leant back against the wall of the bathroom and closed my eyes. What was I going to do? Panic knotted my stomach. I could feel the nausea rising in me again as the smell of the carbolic soap wafted up, and I stood there, cold and shaken, full of apprehension for the future.

There was no way the baby could be passed off as Theo's. The thought had occurred to me, but I gave it no more than a minute's consideration. Everyone could see for themselves that he was doting, and the thought that he could father a child at his age and in his condition was simply not credible. To ask anyone to believe that I would encourage him into bed in his state was even more ridiculous.

There had never been any expectations for me to have children. With Hannah, it was taken for granted that, as soon as she was married, she would start a family. True to form, she and Willie had three fine sons in four years. Then he went to war, leaving her with the farm and three youngsters to look after. He was back in three months minus his left arm, which had been blown away, but he knew, for all that, that he was one of the lucky ones.

Hannah was a natural mother but, while I found her children

a pleasant distraction for a time, I tired of them easily. I found that I had no desire to have any of my own. Perhaps the family saw this in me. They could see I was tied up with the business, and had never expressed any expectation one way or the other as far as children were concerned. With Theo's age, and the fact that he already had a son, it seemed to be taken for granted that I would not have a family. There had been none of the usual banter and teasing about the patter of tiny feet. No, I had been saved all that, and I would have had no patience with it in any case.

I listened at the door of the bathroom, but there was no sound in the corridor. All the housemaids and kitchen staff were busy with their work. With any luck there'd be no ears or eyes alert to my bout of sickness, nor any tongues wagging as to what could be the cause of it.

I went quickly to my office in the yard and closed the door, intending to get on with some paperwork. My mind would not settle. What was I to do? I was in a real pucker by then and I had no one I could turn to. My friends were my family and they would not be able to help me, for they'd be shocked to the core at the thought of my infidelity. I had no close acquaintances to turn to because, between life with Theo, the business and finding opportunities to meet John, I had neither time nor inclination to be with childhood friends. I had nowhere to turn for help. I had considered contacting Lizzy who was working as a doctor in Belfast but I decided that I couldn't involve her as it would put her career at risk.

I knew for sure that I could not have this child, so I would just have to find a way to get rid of it. I had heard about the old wives' tales for ending unwanted pregnancies and I would have to put them to the test. I think at that time I was desperate enough to try anything. If Violet could see that I was overtired then I realised that others would think so too, though they all knew what a handful Theo was. I vowed to take myself off for a hot bath with a bottle of gin that night.

I might as well not have bothered, for all I ended up with was a thick head the next morning. Over the next few weeks, I was aware of Violet watching me. She would never stare, but often as I turned around in the kitchen her eyes would slide off me. She was not obtrusive and there was usually the glint of concern in her expression. I wondered if she knew, but I hoped that if I behaved normally and kept myself well pulled in, I would be able to act out the charade.

Then, one afternoon, she came into my office with the tea tray. I thanked her and smiled at her, but she hesitated beside me, making no shape to leave.

'Are you all right, Mrs Grey? You look so tired these days. I was thinking you should call the doctor and get yourself a tonic. It is getting you run down, all this looking after the master. You look a bit anaemic to me, if you don't mind me saying so.'

'I'll be all right, Violet. I haven't felt great for a while but once the spring comes and better weather is here, I'll pick up again.'

She looked at me, hesitating, and then said slowly,

'Have you seen the doctor recently? About yourself, I mean?'

'No, it's always Theo he comes to see.'

'Well, you might call me a silly old fool and you might tell me to mind my own business, but I have a feeling you might be pregnant,' she said slowly. She must have seen the shock on my face because I could not manage to hide it. I knew she might suspect what was up, but I never thought for a minute she would confront me with it. I sat there speechless.

'Listen, my dear, you're not the first and not the last this has happened to. Sure, it's been going on since time began.' She turned from me then and set out the cup and saucer and poured me a cup of tea. 'Here,' she said, passing it to me. 'Get this down you. It'll make you feel better.' I obeyed her like a child, still unsure quite what to say or how much I should tell her. Could I deny it, I wondered, or bluff her that it was Theo's?

Before I had a chance to decide which way to play it, she pulled up the little chair beside me and said,

'Now listen here. It is not the master's, is it? If it was, you wouldn't be worrying and hiding the way you have done. God love him, he is no more capable of fathering a child than I am. I don't want to interfere or ask your business, but I know I can be of help to you and that's why I'm here.'

For the first time I looked up and met her eyes. I knew I'd never have anything to fear from Violet, for we had worked together over the years and there had always been a real bond of affection between us.

'My sister has a friend, a nurse, who has her own house down on the shores of Carlingford Lough just outside Rostrevor. We could make arrangements for you to go to her and have the child on the quiet. I can help to cover up for you here.'

I could barely speak for a moment, but I realised there was no point in trying to fool Violet and there was no doubt she was trying to do the best for me. I knew I could trust her, and

I needed her, for there was no one else I could rely on.

'Oh, Violet. I just don't know what I am going to do,' I said, fighting the tears that were prickling my eyes. 'One day I think one thing and the next day another. I really am in a stew.'

'Never mind,' she said. 'You know I'll do what I can to help. Between you and me, we had to do this for a niece of mine a couple of years ago and it all went like clockwork. My sister's friend will look after you very well. Just don't be too hard on yourself. Give yourself a bit of a break sometimes. You need it.'

It was at the Spa one warm evening in April that I broke the news to John. As he held me to him, it felt as if all the love in the world surrounded me and I stood in a special golden place of my own. In those days at the Spa, I lived the youth that I left behind when I married Theo. Instead of being the manager, the nurse, the dedicated wife to a man of importance, I could allow my love of fun and my laughter to come out. It was at the Spa that I found I could enjoy the prospect of being a young wife and a mother.

It was bliss to be looked after and indulged. John was the ideal companion – handsome, generous, and with a giddy sense of humour that matched mine perfectly. He took great care of me and was always sure that I had everything I needed. Sometimes he would pull me to him and lay his hand on me to feel the baby. Then his face would light up with wonder when he felt the firm kicks of his child.

I was blooming with health. The days of sickness had gone and the days of tiredness and feeling swollen were yet to come so, in this middle stage of pregnancy, my skin glowed and my hair shone with a heightened gloss. I felt in the peak of condition. I was slowly coming to a decision about my future and I had made up my mind to go. I had paid my dues to Theo – I had repaid tenfold the investment he had put into me. I had given him ten good years of companionship, care and love of a kind, yet I still felt guilty at leaving him and making a life of my own. He was, after all, my husband.

By early summer, the plans for the birth and afterwards were in place. The head gardener at the Spa Hotel lived nearby, and his wife, Ellen, acted as midwife for the local area. She has a reputation that went far and wide, and it was said that all the local doctors deferred to her in cases of difficult pregnancies and births. They had a grown family of their own, but Ellen still had a hankering for taking care of babies.

When I met her, I was reassured by her manner and her knowledge. There was nowhere suitable at the Spa for my final confinement, so we agreed that having the baby in Rostrevor was the best option. It was arranged that Ellen and her family would then foster the child for us until we decided what to do.

There is a saying that troubles never come singly. In the spring of 1919, I had good reason to think there was never a truer saying. I had struggled with the shock of my pregnancy, battled with myself over the issue of abortion, worried about how John would react to it all when I told him the news, and coped with Theo and the business. I did not need anything else to add to my troubles, but life is rarely simple.

It was a morning in April that a letter arrived from the bank manager. When I opened it, I got the biggest shock of my life.

Chapter 19

BANK VISIT

The letter from the bank manager was a complete and utter shock to me. Samuel had taken over the management of the mill from Theo, and had been doing an excellent job – and I knew how well it was performing, as I kept a close eye on things by having a weekly meeting with Samuel and the bookkeeper. During those war years, the economy boomed and many of the businesses in the province benefited. We had the mill working day and night for the war effort, and because it was no longer possible to get flax from German-occupied Belgium, thousands of acres of Ulster grassland had been ploughed to grow it there.

Flax was used to make linen, which had undergone a strong revival before the war and was essential to meet the demand for tents, uniforms, stretchers, kitbags and even aeroplane fabric. We were well placed to get the contracts from the War Office because of Theo's good name, and those who knew of his illness seemed to rally round and make sure that work always came our way. It was not just kind-heartedness – our mills had a reputation for being efficient, and for bringing work in on time and at the quality required.

People knew that, even though Theo was not running the business any more, the work would be as reliable as ever. Even after the war had ended, our mill was just as busy. With all the work coming in, it was a shock on that April morning to find that when I opened the letter from the bank, it said there was an enormous hole in our finances.

I knew where to go to find the answers. Matt Dixon did all the books and he had been working with Theo from the year dot, so he knew every detail of our financial dealings.

He and I did not get along at all well. He resented me, although he was too canny to show it. I knew he thought that I should be like all the other women and stick to the home and the kitchen, just like his own cowed wee wife – but of course he had enough sense not to show his feelings. He made me cringe with his smarmy, solicitous ways and I made sure I had as little to do with him as possible. He loved to make me feel uncomfortable – juvenile, even, but then he was a man who had been born old. Modern ideas about women would never take root in his mind.

Teresa O'Connell greeted me as I came into the office.

'Morning, Mrs Grey.' Her bright smile quickly faded when she saw the look on my face. She was a bright lass and she had been promoted quickly by Theo because of her ability with figures, much to the displeasure of Dixon. He was willing to tolerate Catholics working on the mill floor but not in the office with him. To his mind, that was a position reserved for good loyal Protestants.

'Morning, Teresa,' I replied briskly. 'Is Dixon about?'

'Just down seeing the foreman. He shouldn't be long. Does he know you're coming?'

'No, he's not expecting me, so could you send someone down and let him know I am here. I'll wait in his office.'

‘Can I get you a cup of tea while you wait?’

‘No, I’m fine thanks. I’ll just go on through.’

Dixon’s office was like him, old and fusty. There were shelves of ledgers and records, and his desk was a neat pile of organised papers. I was half tempted to poke into the books for, after all, the responsibility for the business lay with me, but I knew that that would just rile him and caution prevailed.

‘Oh. I wasn’t expecting you, ma’am,’ Dixon said as he entered the office, and in those few words he managed to convey how unwelcome I was.

‘I need some information, Dixon,’ I said, deciding to dispense with any superficial small talk.

‘I’ll try to help all I can. Take a seat,’ he said, offering me a chair.

‘Business is fine, I take it?’

‘Couldn’t be better, ma’am. You know that from our weekly meetings.’

‘Oh, yes. You keep me well informed. That’s why I’m rather surprised at the bank statement this morning.’

‘What do you mean?’

I watched him carefully for any signs of nervousness.

‘I mean the ten thousand pounds that has been withdrawn.’

He furrowed his brow and shook his head.

‘Ten thousand?’ he repeated. ‘What do you mean, ten thousand pounds?’

‘Ten thousand pounds was withdrawn from the account of Blackwater Mills as of yesterday. At the moment, we have nothing in the bank.’

He stood up and stared at me, continuing to shake his head.

‘Is this some kind of joke?’

'You tell me.'

I held his eyes with a long, unblinking stare, but I could see no sign of guilt there, only confusion. Was he covering up or was he as genuinely surprised and confused as he seemed? I could not tell, but my honest reaction was that he was telling the truth, and that he was as shocked as I had been to learn of this large withdrawal from the bank. Yet it seemed impossible, for he knew every detail of the finances. How could he have missed such a large sum?

'I really have to assure you, Mrs Grey, that I have not the slightest clue what all this is about. I am as much in the dark as you are about the money. You say it went out of the account yesterday?'

'Yes, that's right. That's what the letter from the bank manager said.'

'Well now, let me see. I need to check all our outgoings.' He fussed around, searching in a red leather ledger, which he had withdrawn from one of the drawers in his desk. I could see he was confused and in a state of shock. His hands were trembling as he ran his pudgy fingers down columns of figures, muttering to himself under his breath as he did so.

'I just can't see it. There must be some mistake. I know there must be some mistake.' He raised his head and looked at me, pleading with his eyes that there was some other explanation and that he was not being accused in any way.

'I need to check this out right away,' I said. 'I'll go into Armagh and see the bank manager. If anyone has an explanation of this, it will be him.'

'Do you want me to come with you?' he said, cautiously. 'Would that be of any help?'

'I suggest you do a bit more checking and see what you can discover,' I said sharply over my shoulder to him as I left his office.

I got into the car and drove straight to Armagh. At the bank, I went up to the glass partition marked *Enquiries* and gave it a good hard knock, for I was in no mood for any delay. The window was pulled back a few moments later and a bald, bespeckled head peered through and said,

'Yes, ma'am?'

'I want to see Mr Graham immediately,' I said.

'Do you have an appointment?' he asked.

'No. Tell him Mrs Grey from Lindara is here and needs to see him immediately.' He hesitated. 'Just do as I say,' I warned him. 'I need to see him right away.'

'Well, just take a seat a wee minute and I'll see what I can do for you.'

With that, the frosted glass was pulled closed and I heard the thump of his feet on the hard wooden floor as he disappeared down the corridor to the manager's office. I could not sit down. I was in too much of a state to sit still. I walked back and forth in the confines of the small room, unable to stay still or relax while the problem was still unresolved.

There must be some mistake. I was sure that it would all be explained easily, but it seemed strange that such a large figure could have been deducted from our account in error. Still, stranger things had happened.

On the mad drive to Armagh my mind had turned over every possibility for the withdrawal, but none of them made any sense. Dixon had gone through the books, and I was sure that if there had been some easy explanation he could have given it to me.

I did not like the man, but I did not doubt his integrity. If he was going to steal from us, I was sure he was clever enough to do it in a small but steady flow so that we would not notice. I'd come to the conclusion that if he had embezzled that amount of money from the company, he would have disappeared before the bank statement ever reached me and we would, by now, be looking for Dixon as well as the ten thousand pounds.

'Mr Graham will see you now,' the bank clerk said, and he held the door open for me. I passed him and walked on ahead down the corridor to the bank manager's office.

'Come in, Mrs Grey,' he said to greet me. 'Take a seat.'

'Thank you,' I replied as I sat down, showing an outward calm I did not feel inside. 'I need an explanation for the large withdrawal from the account of Blackwater Mills that was made yesterday,' I said, not bothering with any niceties.

'Ah, I thought that might be the reason for your visit.'

'It is hardly a paltry amount, and I have no explanation as to why the withdrawal was made. I'm rather hoping you're going to tell me it's all a mistake, but I can see that you're aware of the withdrawal, so I presume you're going to tell me it's all in order.'

'Yes, indeed,' he nodded. 'I'm afraid it is all in order.'

My heart sank and I suddenly went cold. I could feel my stomach churning.

'How could this be?' I thought to myself. I was so sure it was all going to be a dreadful mistake and now it was as bad as I had imagined.

'But, Mr Graham, I have no knowledge of this, and nor does Mr Dixon. We cannot find any explanation for such a large withdrawal. There's no invoice or debt on the books that relates to that amount.'

He rose and came around the desk to me. He leant down as if he was talking to a child and there was a look of concern in his eyes.

'Did you not know anything about this, Mrs Grey?' he said, and there was genuine mystification in his voice.

'Mr Graham, I can assure you I do not know anything about this money. I do not know who it is being paid to, I don't know what it is paying for, and I'm totally in the dark as to what it's all about. Can you please give me an explanation?' I could hear the strain of it all rising in my voice as I spoke.

He went over to a large safe in the corner of the office, turned the key and clicked the handle, and the heavy door swung outwards without a sound. He rooted around inside for a moment and then returned to his desk with an orange folder. He laid this on his desk and opened it to reveal a thick pile of papers. The document he wanted was at the top and he extracted it deftly. After a quick look to check it, he passed it to me.

The document was an official deed, printed on heavy vellum, complete with an official seal. I looked at it, but at first I was too strung up to take it in. The words danced before me on the page. They did not make any sense and I could not concentrate my mind to read it.

Then, at the bottom, I saw the signatures, clear and legible. They were those of Theo and Lord Clanhugh. I raised my eyes from the page, trying to calm myself. Mr Graham sat across the desk, staring at me and saying nothing.

'Can you just tell me what this means, Mr Graham? I need

to know exactly what it means.'

'It means that Theo has acted as guarantor for the full amount of money that was drawn from your account yesterday. That, in short, means that he has underwritten the debt for ten thousand pounds. Since it was not available in the account controlled by him and Lord Clanhugh, it was deducted from the Blackwater Mills account, as agreed in the document you have in hand.'

I was stunned. Ten thousand pounds. What was Theo thinking of, to guarantee that amount of money? Why were the funds not available in the account of the UVF? For that was the fund that was jointly controlled by Theo and Lord Clanhugh. To my knowledge there was plenty of money in that account. Only a few short years ago there had been enough money to buy large quantities of arms and ammunition from the European suppliers, and now the account was ten thousand in debt.

'I'm afraid, Mr Graham, I need more of an explanation than that. The mill has been doing well, as you know, but we cannot afford to underwrite this amount of money. Surely there must be some mistake?'

Mr Graham sighed.

'I really can't help you much further, Mrs Grey. As you can see, the document you have in your hand is genuine and legal. The bank was due its money and we had no option but to act on the guarantee signed by your husband.'

I looked at the document again and it all looked totally legitimate.

'But Lord Clanhugh's signature is on this document as well. Does that mean he has to forfeit the same amount?'

'The amount guaranteed was ten thousand pounds, and your

husband and Lord Clanhugh are joint guarantors.' I looked at the document again, but it was no clearer than when I had first seen it. The words were making sense to me, now that I had gathered my wits about me, but I couldn't understand why the amount guaranteed was deducted from our account.

'So, if they were both guarantors, I take it then that Lord Clanhugh is liable for half of this amount,' I said.

'In theory, yes.'

'In theory, yes,' I repeated. 'Now, what exactly does that mean, Mr Graham?'

'It means that the amount guaranteed by your husband and Lord Clanhugh was underwritten by them jointly. However, if the funds are not available in one account, the second guarantor becomes fully liable.'

I nodded at him slowly as the picture began to dawn on me as to what had happened.

'So, you're saying that there are no funds in the Clanhugh account to cover the sum, and that therefore Theo becomes the sole guarantor for the full amount?'

'I can't possibly discuss the details of an account of another customer with you. You must realise that it's confidential.' He paused and I could see that he was reluctant to say more, yet I felt he sympathised with my position. 'However, I can say that you're not far wrong in your conclusions.'

So, the Clanhughs were bust. It did not surprise me. There had been rumours around for some time about the state of their finances, and I knew from long experience that any debt they owed would only be paid after many requests for the money and always with poor grace, but then that's just how the Clanhughs were. They always paid up in the end. I did not supply them with any goods or services, and they had no reason to owe me money, but I had heard the rumours.

My mind flew back to that morning of the training camp in 1913, when Lucinda had had to have the best of everything even though the expense was quite unnecessary, in my opinion. I remembered John's words that morning. He knew, even then, that they were hard-pushed. How did he know so much? Surely, he was not involved in any of this.

My mind raced in panic at the thought that he could be at the back of all of it. He certainly had made an enormous amount of money in a few short years, but now I wondered if it was all legitimate. I had doubted him in Dublin when I saw him with his foreign friend, yet he had put my mind at rest on that occasion. Now the doubts rose again. Was there anyone I could trust?

Mr Graham was busy shuffling through the papers in the orange folder, but I could see that it was a diversionary tactic. He was not paying attention to the papers in the file. He was merely playing with them to cover his embarrassment.

'Look, Mr Graham, I realise that you can't discuss the accounts of other people with me, but I really can't understand why there is no money left in the account that Theo and Lord Clanhugh controlled, the UVF account. I mean, they had money galore only a few years ago and, although a lot of it was spent on goods from Europe, Theo would not have spent more than they had. He has always been very prudent in his financial affairs, as you know.'

'Oh, indeed he has,' Mr Graham agreed readily. 'Always very exact and reliable.'

'So, where has the money gone?' I asked.

He looked at me and hesitated, but then protocol and the rules of the bank got the upper hand and I could see his mind closing.

'Sorry, Mrs Grey,' he said, rising from his chair. 'I really cannot discuss this with you any further. When things have settled down, perhaps you could come and see me about the finances for the mill. We need to discuss them further in the light of the debt on the account.'

I rose and followed him, numb and speechless. Had he no feelings after all these years of doing business with the Grey family? I was going to have to come to him to arrange loans to cover our new debt even though we had a history of being a good, hard-earning business with money in the bank. Already I could sense the hardening of his attitude to me.

Even with all that, I was unprepared for his throwaway remark as he left me at the door of the bank.

'Have a word with the son. Maybe he can tell you more,' he said. And then he turned and disappeared as the heavy oak door closed behind him.

Chapter 20

CONFRONTING SAMUEL

Samuel ... what did he have to do with all this? How was he involved? My mind was racing as I drove back to Lindara, trying to puzzle out what Samuel knew.

I thought back to the summer of 1914, when the war started, and all the young lads were joining up. He was barely sixteen that September and, like the others, desperate to go to war when he was old enough. They all had stars in their eyes at that stage and saw only the glory of battle. It was not until the summer of 1916 and the carnage of the Somme that reality struck home, and the young men realised the futility of it all.

By then, I had persuaded Samuel that he was needed at home to help with Theo. He had accepted it with great reluctance even though common sense told him that, with no conscription in Ireland, he didn't need to go. A part of him was still the romantic, wanting to experience the war at first hand, and I wondered now if he had harboured a deeper resentment at my insistence on him staying at home to help me. Was there something in that, which had turned him into a thief?

I was home by teatime, but there was no sign of Samuel. He and Theo were in Dungannon and were not due back until early evening. I got through those hours by keeping myself busy around the hotel, but waiting to hear the car pull into the yard seemed like days to me. I rehearsed in my mind how to approach the subject, how to get the truth from him. I decided it was best to present him with the facts, and ask for a straight and honest explanation.

The lights of the car struck the ceiling of my bedroom, and I knew they were back. By the time I got downstairs Theo was in the kitchen, but there was no sign of Samuel.

'Samuel has gone up to the mill, Mrs Grey,' Violet said. 'He has some stuff to drop off that he picked up in Dungannon, but he said he wouldn't be long. I was just getting Mr Grey his tea.'

'Thanks, Violet. I'll leave you to see to him, if you don't mind. I was just in the middle of something upstairs.' I fussed around Theo and made sure he had his pipe and slippers, and then left him to Violet. It was easier to be on my own than to try and make conversation with anyone. Another hour ticked by, but the car had not pulled into the yard. Where could he be? Then I heard Samuel's voice on the stairs and I realised he must have come back without me noticing.

'There you are, Samuel,' I said, as I met him on the landing. 'I didn't hear the car coming into the yard.'

'No. I ran out of petrol up at the mill and I hadn't got the garage keys with me. Boyd had finished work and gone home, so I had to walk back. I'll see to it in the morning.'

'I need a word with you right away.' He glanced at me, picking up the urgency in my voice.

'Sure. I'll be with you in a minute.'

'My study,' I said, as I passed him.

I laid all the facts out before him. I watched him as he paced up and down in my study, so young and guileless. He made to interject from time to time, but I forced him to wait until I'd finished.

'You must be codding me, Sarah.'

'Believe me, Samuel, I've never been more serious in my life.'

'I don't believe you. Tell me it's only a bad joke.'

'It's no joke, Samuel. The money is gone, and the bank says it's all above board and legal as far as our account is concerned.'

'And Dixon doesn't know anything about it?'

'He says not.'

'How can we find out where the money from the UVF account has gone?' He turned to me sharply. 'What about John? He might know about what became of the funds. He was well into the money side of things, with all his dealings on the Continent.'

'I haven't had time to contact him yet,' I said, still watching Samuel closely. If he knew anything about the money or where it had gone, he was a damn good actor. He'd shown nothing but surprise and incredulity as all the facts had been revealed to him.

I looked at him, and the thought that he was bound up in this, in some kind of dishonesty, just didn't seem possible to me. He had always been such a decent, straightforward lad. How could he have stolen such a large sum of money and why would he want to? He had everything he needed in Lindara and he stood to inherit a substantial sum of money when he was twenty one, which would make him a very wealthy person.

'What are we going to do, Sarah?' he asked, in quiet desperation. I drew in my breath and faced him full square. His gaze unwavering, he looked me straight in the eye.

'The thing is, Samuel, as I left the bank Mr Graham told

me that if I wanted to know more, I should speak to you. He said that you would be able to help me.'

He looked at me in puzzlement.

'Me?' he said. 'He said to speak to me? What on earth does he mean by that? I know no more about this than you do.'

'Well, that's not what he implied,' I persisted. 'He said, "Have a word with the son."'

The minute the words left my lips I knew. It hit me with a gut-wrenching certainty and it all fell into place – the Clanhughs, Lucinda's extravagance, and their lifestyle, which had barely changed even with the war.

The thing that nailed it was 'the settlement' that Theo, in his dotage, had been jabbering on about for this past year or more. His words rang in my ears, for he had repeated them often enough to Hugh when he saw him – and so constantly that we all ignored what he said as the ramblings of his mind and not something to pay any attention to.

'The settlement. There will have to be a settlement, Hugh.'

Now it all made sense, and I knew that Samuel was genuine when he said he knew nothing about it. I, in my panic, had been asking the wrong son.

Chapter 21

CONFRONTING HUGH

Lindara House lay bathed in the silver light of a full moon. We stopped at the point where the drive opened out, and our moonlit shadows stretched long across the lawn. I shivered because I had only a thick cardigan on and the night was cold, just verging on being frosty. I had followed Samuel out into the darkness, thinking that he was just going to walk off his anger and frustration, and it was only when he reached the edge of the village and turned in at the gates of Lindara House that I realised his intentions.

'What do you think you're doing?' I asked him, catching him by the arm. He pulled away and turned to face me.

'Going to have it out with that bastard Hugh. What do you think I'm doing?' He turned and stalked off up the drive.

'Wait, Samuel. Just talk this through first. We need to be absolutely sure about Hugh before we confront him. We need to get our facts straight.'

'He's the one who will give us the facts, Sarah. I'm just going to make sure we get them from him before he has a chance to cover up.'

'But what if he turns nasty? You know what Hugh is like when his temper is up.'

'Listen, Sarah,' he said, grabbing me by the arm, 'if this

money isn't sorted, we're ruined. Hugh isn't going to get away with this, temper or no temper.'

He turned then and walked away from me, and I had no choice but to follow. I would normally have enjoyed the walk in the night air. I would have taken in the sharp, fresh spring smells and the movements and sounds of the nocturnal animals, but I was too preoccupied with our problems and keeping up with Samuel to appreciate them that night.

As I struggled to keep up with him, I worried about all Theo's business affairs. His decline had come upon us relatively slowly and, with Samuel running things, the business had gone on as before. Dixon had the authority to sign documents and he dealt with all the daily finances. The difficulty was that, legally, I had no power over Blackwater Mills Company Limited. Theo had not signed the necessary documents to give me power of attorney, and I had no legal standing to carry on the business in his name. By the time we realised the need for official paperwork to give me the necessary authority, Theo's mind was too far gone, and he would not have been legally capable of signing it.

We had struggled through these last few years on the goodwill and understanding of the bank manager, but my legal situation was in limbo. The manager understood the importance of keeping the mill running, producing goods for the war effort, and maintaining jobs for all the local workers. The hotel was not a problem, as I had full legal control of its finances. The things that caused the real difficulties were the other external matters that Theo had been involved in.

I had no authority to deal with third parties. The control of the UVF account was a perfect example of a situation where Theo was still responsible on paper, but could not act on his own behalf and no one was designated to act for him. In a few months' time we would be out of the woods. Arrangements had been made some years ago for Samuel to take responsibility for running the mill and Theo's other affairs on his twenty-first birthday. For now, though, we were in trouble.

The house was almost in darkness. A dull yellow light flowed out across the gravel from the front room at the far end of the house. It was a family sitting room and was used most evenings when they were at home. Two small dormer windows in the roof were also lit with the soft flicker of a candle. On the east wing of the house, there was a light in two of the windows on the ground floor, the last two towards the back of the house.

'Hugh's in the gunroom,' Samuel said, after pausing for a minute to take in the evidence of the illuminated windows.

He strode off down the side of the house. There was a steel and a determination in him that I had rarely seen before but had always suspected was there. He stopped briefly at the back door, and then turned the knob and opened it. The debris of the family life of the Clanhughs was scattered around – coats and hats on the hangers along the walls, and boots in various shapes and sizes stacked in untidy rows underneath.

Samuel moved down the corridor and knocked impatiently on the first door on the left. He did not wait for a reply but walked straight in. The gunroom had been the private retreat of generations of Clanhughs. It was old and worn, and there was nothing grand about it, yet there was a comfort in it that many of them must have relished in their private moments, when they needed to relax, away from the rigours and demands of public life. At the back of the room, behind the desk, there was a gun cabinet filled with a selection of shotguns. Next to that was a rod cabinet, and a variety of spinners and reels lay on the shelf. There was a print of a grouse moor on the wall. Well-thumbed dusty old books on country life and pursuits filled the bookshelves that lined the rest of the room. It was a male retreat that had never been touched or altered by any female over the years.

'Samuel,' I heard Hugh exclaim. 'You gave me a fright, coming in on the quiet like that. To what do I owe the honour at this time of night?'

I stepped into the doorway.

'Sarah too,' he said, as his eyes fell on me.

Poacher, his old black Labrador, rose on his arthritic legs and ambled over to greet me. He nuzzled against my shins and I gently stroked his greying head. I watched Hugh as I petted the dog, for I knew from the tone of his voice that he had been drinking. A bottle of claret and a half-empty glass sat on the desk. He was not drunk but he wasn't completely sober, either. I knew from experience that Hugh could easily turn nasty after a few drinks and I quietly prayed that Samuel would go easy on him.

'Strange time of night to come calling without a word of warning. What's the problem?' he asked in a truculent voice. Not for the first time in my life I wondered about Hugh's sensitivity to the world around him. He had missed all the cues of Samuel's mood and body language. If he had picked them up he showed no sign, for his attitude showed not a hint of conciliation or concern, yet it was very obvious to anyone who cared to be observant that Samuel could barely control his temper.

'We need to talk,' Samuel said tersely.

Hugh raised his eyebrows as if to question the statement and then thought better of it.

'You'd better have a seat, then,' he said, motioning me to the chair by the desk. 'There's one in the corner for you, Samuel.'

'I'm fine. I'll stand,' Samuel replied.

I sat upright on the front edge of the chair because I wanted to be able to control Samuel if his temper got the better of him. I picked nervously at my nails, a habit that I had tried hard to stop but which always came back in anxious moments.

'Sarah had a shock this morning. There was a letter from the bank informing her that ten thousand pounds has been transferred to underwrite a debt to the UVF account. It appears your father and Theo were joint signatories on a guarantee for the account. It came due two days ago.' Samuel paused while Hugh sat completely still with a small frown on his face.

'So, that's what you've come about, is it? Couldn't it wait till morning?'

'No. I want an explanation here and now, not next week or next month.'

'Steady, Samuel,' I said, as calmly as I could. 'Don't rile him or you'll get nowhere.'

'You know about the guarantee, I take it?' Samuel asked.

'I do, yes,' he replied.

'What do you intend to do about honouring your half of it?' Samuel asked.

Hugh paused and held his stare for a moment. Then he looked away as he lifted the glass of wine and took a long drink. He had not offered us anything to drink, but then the situation was hardly one for social niceties.

'I'm afraid there's a problem there,' he replied eventually.

'What exactly do you mean?' Samuel asked gruffly.

He looked at me and then at Samuel, and when he spoke a new hardness had come into his voice.

'What I mean is, there are no funds available in the Lindara estate accounts to cover this guarantee.'

We stared at each other and then at Hugh, whose demeanour was haughty and defiant.

'Hugh,' I said, 'the guarantee is in both names – Theo's and your father's – and you, as your father's heir, are responsible for the guarantee. I checked this out with my solicitor today. You inherited the debt, just as you inherited the estate and all the assets.'

'Ha, ha, ha,' he snorted. He laughed, but it was a forced laugh, lacking in mirth. Samuel and I could only watch him with growing consternation. He was surprised to see us arrive at this time of night, but he wasn't surprised by what we had to say. It was as if he had been waiting for it. He had known that, sooner or later, the whole thing would come out in the open and that we would have to have it out. It was Samuel and I who were at the disadvantage, still shocked by the news, whereas Hugh had had a long time to mull it over, to plan exactly what he was going to do.

I tried to remain calm, but I knew already that he was way ahead of us. He'd had a long time to cover his tracks. Hugh had had control of the state estate since probate was completed on his father's will more than two years earlier and, as the sole beneficiary, he'd gained access to all his father's accounts and business papers. He would have known all about the guarantee, and the fact that he had not made provision for it indicated to me that he had no intention of doing so.

He also had access to the money in the UVF account and had, in effect, been the sole controller of it over the last two years. With Theo unable to look after the UVF affairs and the movement's voluntary suspension of all its activities during the war, the account had languished, building up interest. At least that is what I had assumed until this morning.

'So, are you saying you cannot stand your part of the guarantee?' I asked.

'I'm afraid that's the position at the moment,' he mumbled, looking past me to the bookshelves behind me. I stared straight at him, but he refused to look me in the eye.

I hesitated.

'You say, "at the moment." Do you mean there will be funds available in the near future?'

'That's not clear, Sarah.'

'What do you mean, it's not clear? If the funds are not available now, when will they be available?' Samuel asked, his voice rising.

Hugh cleared his throat and looked away. He moved uneasily in his chair.

'It's not clear just now. I just really don't know.'

Samuel and I stared at him in horror. It was worse than we thought. Not only did he not have the funds for his part of the guarantee, but he seemed to have no idea when he could pay his debt.

'Tell me, Hugh,' I said quietly, 'where did the funds from the UVF account disappear to?' I watched him as he tightened his hand on the glass. His eyes darted round the room and his head bobbed nervously.

‘What do you mean, Sarah?’

‘Well, it’s obvious that the funds in the account have been depleted, otherwise the bank would not have needed to call on the guarantee.’ I hesitated, watching him. I could see the anger rising in him, but I had to press to get the truth. I could not just back off because of his temper. ‘Since your father died, and with Theo the way he is, you’re the only one to have access to the account. No one else could have removed money except you.’ I waited with Samuel tense beside me.

‘We had to pay off a lot of the movement’s debts last year,’ he blustered. ‘Theo and Father had agreed shipments that had to be paid for.’

I knew he was lying. I knew from Theo and I knew from John that no shipment had been made since 1914. The gentleman’s agreement to suspend operations for the duration of the war had been totally enforced.

‘You have paperwork for the payments?’ I asked, playing along with his lie.

‘Yes,’ he replied. ‘Of course. The paperwork is confidential, you appreciate that. I am not in a position to let you or Samuel see it.’

‘How very convenient,’ Samuel said quietly, his voice full of sarcasm.

‘Now that’s enough,’ Hugh shouted, bolting from his seat. The glass of wine spilt across the top of the desk. ‘You come in here uninvited at the dead of night and then accuse me of misusing funds. Just get out, both of you.’

He moved round the desk towards Samuel.

‘We’re not going without the answers we came for,’ Samuel shouted at him.

'Calm down, both of you,' I cried out.

They stood eye to eye.

'Tell us what we need to know, you bastard,' Samuel snarled.

Hugh grabbed him.

'Get out, you little shit. Get out of my house this minute or I'll throw you out.'

Samuel pushed him. Hugh rocked back and lost his balance, falling heavily against the side of the desk. I saw the grimace of pain as his face went red. He heaved himself to his feet and swung at Samuel. I yelled at them both to stop but they were at each other, fists flying. I pulled at them, but they took no notice. Poacher stood, his tail erect, growling.

Hugh pushed Samuel away and turned from him. The glass of the cabinet caught the light as it swung open. In a swift movement Hugh lifted the shotgun off the shelf and swung it round. In the small room it was inches from Samuel's chest. Samuel swung his arm and knocked the gun upwards towards the ceiling. Then he lurched forward and was on Hugh, pulling and clawing.

'Leave him. Just leave him,' I screamed, as I pulled at Samuel's arm. He stepped back and his elbow struck me in the stomach, and I curled up in pain. As I lifted my head, I saw that Samuel had the gun. I pulled at his arm again, then my hand went forward to the gun.

Then the room exploded. For a long moment the sound filled the room, echoing and bouncing, booming into and through and round my head. Then there was total silence, a long, ringing silence that went on and on. The taste and the smell of cordite stung deep in my throat and a curling plume of smoke rose slowly to the ceiling, doing a slow dance of death as it melted into nothing.

Hugh fell backwards into his chair, a large wound spurting blood from his neck and head. It spread in a deep red stain down his chest and onto the cover of the chair. Samuel stood still, the shotgun dangling in his hand.

Poacher gave a low growling moan and licked his master's motionless hand. The two of us watched without moving, transfixed with horror. I knew there was nothing I could do for Hugh and I could only stand and watch as his life slipped away. Samuel stood beside me, immobile, his face white with shock, and then slowly his whole body began to shake.

'Let's go. Now. Before the servants come,' I said urgently. He dropped the gun at my command. As we went through the door, we could hear shouting at the far end of the house and the thud of running feet. We were out and across the lawn into the bushes in seconds. I led the way, running through the trees to a woodland path that led to the village by a roundabout route.

Within half a mile I stumbled from the burning agony in my belly. I almost cried out in pain but then stopped myself. Samuel must not know about the baby. Not now, not ever.

'We'll have to slow down,' I gulped through strained breaths. 'I need to rest.'

'Oh, Sarah, what will we do?' Samuel wailed as he caught up with me. 'I never meant for that to happen.'

'I know. I know. Don't worry, we'll think of something,' I consoled him.

We rested until the throbbing pain in my belly subsided and then we started out again.

'Get your shoes off,' I ordered Samuel as we reached the river. He obeyed me mechanically. The cold of the water sent piercing pains up my legs.

I went carefully, making sure with each step that I had a sound foothold on the rocky bottom of the river, but trying to hurry to ease the agony of the cold. I was safely across when I heard a deep flop, and looked around expecting to see him in the river.

'Bloody shoe,' he exclaimed.

'Shush. There might be someone about. For God's sake make sure the other one doesn't go in.' He scooped the shoe up from the riverbed and poured the water out of it. In a moment we were both on the riverbank and we struggled to fit our shoes and socks back onto our cold, wet feet. I was glad of the momentary rest, for the pain in my belly was sharp and stabbing. We skirted the edge of the field, not risking crossing open ground in the bright moonlight. In another ten minutes we were out onto the road on the north side of the village.

'We can't hide from here on. It would be better if we walk openly on the road. If anyone sees us, we were up at the mill and the car broke down. Is that clear, Samuel?'

'Yep,' he replied. His eyes looked blank and cold in the grey moonlight. 'At least if anyone checks they'll find that the car did run out of petrol and had to be left at the mill. It could be just the alibi we need.'

Within five minutes we were safely back in the yard of the hotel.

'Act as normally as you can. We'll talk this over tomorrow, but for now we have to be as natural as possible.' I pushed him through the door in the direction of the back staircase, hoping he would get to his room without anyone seeing him.

After closing the door of my room, I kicked off my shoes and slumped on the bed. My body sagged slowly, like a deflating balloon, and I curled up around the life that was already moving inside me, as if to protect it from all the harm that could come from the evil world outside. I covered my eyes but the image of Hugh with the blood running down his chest was there, etched in my mind. I knew it was an image that would stay with me to the end of my days.

I could not cry. It might have been better if I had done, as it would have been a release. I could only lie there, trying to warm myself, shaking with fear and shock, and worrying about what was to become of us and how we would cover up our crime.

'Could I have prevented this?' I asked myself time and time again as I reviewed the events leading up to that night. If I had not been spending time away from Lindara seeing John, could I have picked up on this problem and done something about it? If I had kept a much closer eye on Hugh, perhaps this whole tragedy could have been prevented.

The guilt I felt at my affair and my pregnancy made me blame myself for all the rest of the mess. Yet I couldn't have known of this debt, for I had no access to any of the papers relating to the movement. Could I have stopped Samuel going up to confront Hugh?

My mind went around in circles, making sure there was no chance of sleep. And then I did something I had not done for many a long year. I prayed.

Chapter 22

TIT FOR TAT

Five days later Sean O'Connell was shot dead. His body lay in a ditch until daylight, when it was found by one of the millworkers. They called a tit-for-tat murder. Tit for tat – a simple phrase, said as if it was a child's game that was being played. I do this and you do that – tit for tat, tit for tat.

That sort of swift, brutal retribution was not uncommon. Sean O'Connell and his clan had strong Republican sympathies, and their Sinn Fein activities were widely talked about. He was blamed for Hugh's murder, and it did not matter if he was the actual murderer or not. He was the head of the local Republican group and he was held responsible. Retribution had to be quick and lethal.

The Sinn Feiners were causing a bit of a stir by then, ever since the Easter Rising of 1916 in Dublin and the subsequent martyrdom of the men who'd led the insurrection. Many of the Catholic community were attracted to violence as a means of achieving an island that was undivided and free from British rule, and who could blame them? They had seen how the threat of violence had helped the Protestant cause.

By early in 1919 there were all sorts of disagreements about the division of Ireland – whether there would be a border and where it would go. It was of great importance to people like us living in the area of dispute along the border, for we could have ended up in Ireland or Northern Ireland, have been Irish or British. This caused a lot of arguments and ill will between local Catholics and Protestants. The countryside was seething with bitterness at that time.

For the first few weeks, Samuel and I thought we were in the clear. The murder of Hugh Clanhugh was laid clearly at the door of Sean O'Connell and there were no further investigations. There had, of course, been the initial questions by the local constabulary, but we were ready for that. Sergeant Bowness and his men came from Armagh to question almost everyone in the village and, sure enough, someone had seen Samuel and me returning to the village that night and they commented on it to the police.

It seemed a stroke of luck that Samuel had run out of petrol that night and had left the car up at the mill. It was a simple explanation that was easily checked. Someone else at the mill mentioned that I had been seen burning clothes on the morning after the murder, but Samuel explained that oil had poured down his trousers and shirt when he went to get a can of petrol from the store. The oil was impossible to remove so the clothes had to be burnt. Why would anyone think for a moment that Samuel would have blood on his clothes?

One of the girls had even mentioned his wet shoe. Samuel's explanation was that he had to wash oil off his shoes as well. It was all so plausible.

It was a case of the guilty being assumed innocent. There is no reason on this earth why Samuel and I would be in any way involved with shooting Hugh – we were friends, and had been for life. There were too many other people to blame for us to be even considered as culprits.

With the rifts and divisions that were brewing in the whole of Ireland at that time, and the political hatred, a political motive was the first one thought of and the last one settled on. Sergeant Bowness and his men were sure that the Clanhugh murder had been resolved with O'Connell's killing, and they wrote up their reports and closed the case. They made little further effort to investigate and it fizzled out in no time.

We thought we had heard the end of it. Keeping the mill going after the large drain of cash was our priority. We knew we had little chance of seeing any of our money back from the Clanhugh estate. There were no funds there to repay the debt and, even if there had been, I knew our chances of persuading Lucinda to part with money were slim. She took off to England immediately after the funeral, and none of us expected to see much of her at Lindara in the future. She made her feelings plain on that account.

In a way, the financial problems at the mill proved a diversion for Samuel. He had to concentrate all his efforts on processing the orders that were coming in and keeping the place running, and fortunately this gave him no time to dwell on that night in April. I watched him carefully, waiting for some kind of reaction or breakdown.

We did not talk about it much. We both knew we had to support each other, but we did that in the little things of everyday life without having to put our thoughts into words. There are always too many eyes and ears in a small community, and we knew it was best to put it behind us and carry on. Sometimes I would whisper to him,

'Least said, soonest mended,' when he got agitated, and it seemed to calm him. At other times I would hold him while he cried on my shoulder, great dry, heaving sobs of deep regret.

The warm days of late spring came and went. The may blossom bloomed like white eiderdowns on the hedges, and the fields of apple trees produced their annual display of pink-tinged blossom like the clouds of a summer sunset. The sunshine lifted my spirits and it seemed that the nightmares of the last year were beginning to recede, but I had a long way to go to find peace.

The financial mess at the mill took up much of my time, while Theo was as demanding as ever in his daily routines. The need to win new business for the mill meant frequent visits to Belfast, and I was glad of that.

In Lindara, I had to bind my body in tight corsets to conceal my condition, as I was swelling rapidly with the growing baby. I never worried for an instant about the child, for it was strong and vigorous from the start, letting me know it had a mind of its own. In Belfast I could wear loose clothes to cover up my swelling stomach, but even then I could have run into someone from Armagh, so I could never really relax and let my defences slip. I made sure to stay well away from Malone Road and my uncle's offices in Belfast, so as not to be spotted by the family.

After Hugh's murder everything had to be reassessed again. No longer sure what the future held for me, I could only think from day to day. That day in Carrick I had been resolved to stay with Theo and then, when the baby was on the way, I had thought I would go.

Now my plans to leave Lindara were still unclear. I was needed more than ever at home, at the mill, for Theo, and especially for Samuel. I had been living for the day I could move to Carrick, but now I did not know if it would ever be possible. It seemed that everything was conspiring to keep me there, to bind me to Theo and Lindara.

It was a night in June when Samuel rushed into my study, wild-eyed and shaking with fear.

'What is it?' I asked immediately. He gulped and slumped into an armchair, unable to speak, but I could see from his shaking and his colour that he was petrified. 'Just calm yourself. Here, let me get you a brandy.'

'No, Sarah. You know I hate the stuff.'

'I know, but you have had some kind of shock. It will do you good,' I said, as I poured a glass of cognac. He sipped it and winced at the taste. The glass shook as he lowered it to the table. 'Now, what is it?' I asked gently.

'Is there anyone about?' he whispered. 'Can you check the yard?'

'Don't worry. No one will hear you if you keep your voice low.'

'No. Check the yard first,' he said, and I knew then that his fear ran deep. I lifted the small bin beside my desk and went across to the rubbish tip at the far side of the yard behind the old stable block, looking around carefully as I went. The lights in the kitchen were on and I could hear the noise of the pots and pans being scrubbed and put away after the evening meal. There was nobody about. I closed the door behind me and told Samuel it was all clear but to keep his voice down.

He looked at me with fear in his eyes and said,

'They know.'

'Who knows?' I whispered.

'They know who did it.'

'Samuel, just take your time and tell me from the beginning what has happened.'

He took a deep breath and started.

'I was walking back from Tullycross. One of the O'Connells and Dan Braniff just came at me out of nowhere. They had been waiting for me in the branches of the big oak at Murray's crossroads. They just lit on me, Sarah, and I knew it was me they were out to get. Jesus, they scared the shit out of me.'

He stopped for a moment to collect his thoughts and then lowered his voice to a whisper.

'They knew it was me, that I killed Hugh. They knew that there was money owing between us and that I had good reason to want him dead. Then they said that I had been seen on the night of the murder coming back from the mill, and they reckoned I had taken the long way around through the woods and onto the mill road. God, Sarah, it was as if someone had sat there and watched our every move. How could they know so much?'

I realised then, without a doubt, that time was running out for us. If they could pin the murder to us that night, there was no doubt that our days were numbered.

'How could they know so much, Sarah? I mean, the police believed our story.'

I shook my head at his naivety.

'The police wanted to believe us, Samuel. Bowness is such a decent sort that he could not think we would be mixed up in any of this. Their minds were set on the Sinn Feiners as the culprits and they didn't even want to look beyond that. And dear knows, there are enough Sinn Feiners around to fix the blame on.'

'So how did those two get onto us?'

I shook my head in despair.

'The trouble is, Samuel, that in a village like this the walls have ears. You think you can get away with something but there is always someone there watching you, seeing what you are up to.' I turned to him, and anger swelled up in me as the thought of Teresa O'Connell came to mind.

'I have no doubt where the information on the money troubles came from. And to think that Theo and I were trying to build bridges, to give that girl a chance, and all we got was a nosey bloody traitor in our midst. If I had known, she would never have seen the inside of our office in her life.' We were both silent for a moment, grappling with the enormity of the danger we were both in.

'I suppose the fact that we were out that night because of the car breaking down was a reasonable excuse. Burning the clothes was easy to explain as well, but when they added it to the money problems, they must have concluded that it was me,' Samuel said slowly.

I stopped in front of him and saw that he had not seen the depth of the danger he was in. He had not considered it from their point of view. I spoke carefully, not wanting to make him more frightened than he already was.

'Don't forget the essential bit. They know that their side didn't do it.' I waited for it to sink in, but Samuel was in such a state that he was slow on the uptake. 'They know they didn't do it, and that is more than the police know. The police were easily fobbed off, but O'Connell and his gang knew that Clanhugh was not a target for them. They must have spent the last few weeks checking it out and making sure nobody on their side was responsible.'

I turned away from him to hide the worry on my face and I blamed myself for not thinking it through more carefully. Why hadn't I seen this coming?

Samuel was quiet for a moment.

'Sarah, we had every reason to think we were in the clear. After all the questioning and then the murder of O'Connell, it seemed that both sides had had their go and that was the end of it. It all seemed settled. Even if we had foreseen this, what could we have done about it?'

'What indeed?' I asked myself. There had been so much to worry about these last few weeks that I had not even thought of this as a possibility, and now I had made my plans and they did not involve Samuel. Not only did they not involve him, but the success of my plans depended on Samuel being here in Lindara to carry on the responsibilities I was leaving behind.

Now, everything had changed. Samuel was under threat, and, if anything happened to him, I would never be able to leave. Theo could never manage on his own, not even with the help of Violet, the Colonel and the servants.

There was no doubt in my mind that Samuel was in the most precarious situation and his safety came first. Whatever needed to be done to protect his life would be done, irrespective of my needs.

I had to think of Theo too, and if Samuel had to go, I had to stay. The baby was next on my list of priorities, with John and me at the bottom. There was never any doubt that, even though I had sinned in carrying on my love affair, the needs of Samuel and Theo – both weak and vulnerable – would come first.

I knew too, without asking, that John would support me absolutely and without question.

Chapter 23

SAMUEL UNDER THREAT

Do you know what it is like to live with fear? Not just being worried or anxious, not just a little bit of fear, but a deep terror of what might happen. It is the terror of not knowing if, or when, or how the bullet will come.

Would it be without warning? Would there be a quick, clean execution or would there be torture? Would the torture be long and slow or would it be the traditional kind of tarring and feathering? Or kneecapping? Would you see the signs of it beforehand, or would they just come for you in the dark of night, without warning?

It is worse than the fear of the condemned man. He at least knows his fate, and has the chance to come to terms with it and prepare himself for the end. The fear that we had was of never knowing if an end would come.

We all hope that we will be courageous in the face of death. We imagine the heroic, determined attitude – facing the end with steely fortitude, unflinching and unafraid. Let me tell you, those are the acts of characters in novels and reality is very different. We were frightened, anxious, agitated and cowardly.

I don't pride myself on how I felt in those weeks when we lived with the threat hanging over us. Samuel and I both took all the normal precautions we could. We varied our routines, took different routes to the mill and into Armagh, changed the times at which we did things, and as far as possible broke with any standard schedule. We knew it was just for show because, if they were out to get us, they would choose the time and place and there would be no escape for either of us.

I don't know if I would have been more resolved and less cowardly if I had not been pregnant. The baby inside me changed everything in my life so much, because there was more than just me at stake. On top of that, there was a new dimension to what I wanted from life, now that the baby was growing within me and making its presence felt. I wanted to be there for it, to nourish and protect it. I had a new purpose in life, one that arose outside of me and my needs – and one which made me vulnerable.

I had not been threatened directly. It was Samuel who'd had the first-hand encounter with the Sinn Feiners and my name had not been brought into it. Yet surely they knew that I had been with Samuel that night because we came back into the village together. If Samuel was a suspect for the murder so was I, but I had not been mentioned or threatened, as Samuel had been. I had no idea how much I was implicated in their minds. From what they told Samuel and the conclusions they had drawn from their various sources, it seemed that only Samuel was under the threat of death.

I worried about him. We had become so close over the last years, the caring for Theo and working at the business drawing us together. We were almost the same age, and were as devoted as sister and brother. The escapades we had when learning to drive together and the night we had gone to Larne to collect the guns for the UVF had forged a deep friendship.

I loved him almost as much as John. What would I do if he was murdered? How would I cope without him? It wasn't just his help with Theo that I appreciated, but also his small acts of kindness, his cheerful smile and his sunny good nature, which brightened up the long days in Lindara. Yet I had planned to abandon him.

He was the future of Blackwater Mills and he was due to inherit in less than a year's time. His life was clearly based in Lindara. But for me, once Theo was gone, there was no reason to stay. Samuel would inherit the hotel as well as the mill and, if he married, there would be a question mark over my future, especially if his wife and I did not agree. Theo had provided for me financially, but even that was in doubt now that the mill was in so much debt.

I thought that it wouldn't be long before Samuel married, and things would change between us. There were rumours of a sweetheart, the kind of rumours you pick up from the servants, but which Samuel had never mentioned to me, even on the night he was threatened. He merely said he was walking back from Tullycross when the men came at him, yet he never mentioned a girl or why he had been there. I respected his reticence and didn't question him. If he had a sweetheart who he was serious about, I would meet her when he was ready.

Samuel lived through those weeks in a lather. He did all the things I told him, but he knew that, if they wanted to get him, they would. What we didn't understand was why they hadn't killed him that night. Why did they just threaten him, if they knew that he was Clanhugh's murderer? Did they not want revenge for Sean O'Connell?

To say that they were giving him the benefit of the doubt because they were suspicious but had no proof did not make sense. They never usually stopped to take that kind of care. Rumours were enough for the death sentence, never mind fair play or proof.

What made things worse was the miasma of suspicion that hung over the hotel and the mill. I knew we'd been betrayed by those around us, by the people we employed. Someone close to us had mentioned to the police that Samuel's shoe was wet, and that I had burnt clothes on the morning after the murder. Someone who lived among us, and who was fed and paid by us.

Surely they could have kept the doubt to themselves. Did they not feel enough affection for us to give us the benefit of the doubt? Yet, I could not speak of it to any of them. I could not ask them or put the record straight. I couldn't wheedle out of them who said what or what the police had asked them. We had to carry on, side by side, doing our usual day's work but with a new distance and distrust between us. It mattered less when the police had packed up their bags and gone, and we had been cleared, but the thought of it gnawed at me like a bad toothache.

The thing that cut me most was that it was the inside information about the company finances that had put them on to Samuel. I had no doubts that the information about the money had come from Teresa O'Connell. She was part of the family and she was the only one who could have told them.

It had been accepted practice for many years that we employed Catholics – and we had little choice in a village where the population was half Catholic and half Protestant – but there was an unwritten rule that the Catholics only got the lower, more menial jobs.

It had been breaking new ground to take Teresa into the office, but I had pushed Theo to give her a try because I saw her talent. Old prejudices are often broken down with time and experience, and I knew she would prove her worth. Theo had done it as a result of my persuasion and very much against the will of Dixon, but she had indeed proven herself over the years. Now, I lived to regret it.

I found that I avoided the mill, for I couldn't bear to speak to her or even to look at her. I vowed I would find a reason to remove her in the future, but this was not the time. To sack her now would only make the situation worse, but I swore that she would not get away with her betrayal and continue to get her livelihood from me. The time would come when I would make my move.

The Clanhugh estate was also closed to me, not through any ban on the part of the family, but through my own choosing. Lucinda had decided to live in England with her son, and she employed a manager to run the estate. It had an empty feel to me now that the family members I had known were dead.

I walked daily now, knowing that exercise was particularly important to me in my pregnancy, but after Hugh's death I couldn't bear to walk on Clanhugh land. It broke my heart because I'd grown up wandering the woods of the estate – I loved every inch of it and knew it as well as my own body – but I never put a foot on the estate from that day on.

Chapter 24

SAMUEL LEAVES

It was Samuel's idea to go. I know it was not mine. I need not say that the thought had not occurred to me, for that would be a barefaced lie – I had thought of shunting Samuel off to England or America many times – but I could never bring myself to suggest it, even though it was the obvious thing to do.

He had been threatened again one night in the early part of July, when the marching season was starting and tempers were heating up. He thought that his leaving would only be for a while, until things calmed down. I knew it would be for a lot longer, for the situation was not that simple. I knew that we were drifting towards a decision that would be important and far reaching, but we did it in the way that most decisions are reached – bit by bit, one step at a time, until the conclusion is arrived at.

'It's a way out for me, Sarah,' Samuel said quietly.

I rose from the table and lifted the steaming kettle from the hob, then put the iron ring carefully back in the groove, covering up the glowing red coals that would normally have been banked up for the night.

'I know,' I said, not turning from the range.

'How will you cope on your own?'

'I don't know, Samuel. I'm not going to say it will be easy, but I'll be all right. I'll have to cope.' We were both silent, turning the thing over in our minds, trying to see what the implications would be.

'It'll be just for a while, Sarah, until all this dies down.'

He sat there for a moment, and then he added, in a voice that was eaten away by anguish,

'I can't go on living here with this threat hanging over me, day in and day out, never knowing when they'll come for me. If only I could get away for a while until it all calms down and they forget about it.'

I moved over and put an arm around his shoulders, holding him to me, his head resting on the round of my bosom like a child. He leant on me as if I could give him the strength he needed. We stayed like this for a while and then he lifted his head and looked at me, his blue eyes frightened.

'I never meant to hurt him, Sarah. You know that, don't you?'

'Of course, I do,' I replied quickly, and then gave him a tight hug of confirmation. 'I know you never meant any harm. I was there. I saw for myself what he could do and how his temper was up. It was an accident, an accident.'

'I'll never forgive myself. I know that I will have to live with this until the day I die.' I was silent, just holding him and letting him be. 'I mean, how was I to know that revenge would be taken, and O'Connell would be killed?'

'Of course not, Samuel. None of us could have known that would happen and, from what I hear, Sean O'Connell had it coming to him. They were only too glad of an excuse.'

'God. What a mess.' We were silent for a minute and then I moved slowly away from him and sat down at the table. 'Do you think I'm a coward, Sarah?'

I was firm in my response because I knew he needed reassurance. 'You're no coward. You'd be a fool not to be frightened in this situation. I should know. I've felt damn scared myself these last few weeks.'

He sat upright as if I'd struck him.

'Sarah, of course you have. Here I am thinking of myself and not thinking of you at all.' Then he leant over and took my hand, adding, 'I honestly don't think you have anything to worry about. Even if they saw you with me on the road, it's me they suspect and it's me who they've threatened. Your name was never mentioned. They don't seem to think you had any part in it.'

'I wish I could feel as much confidence as you do,' and as I said it, I felt limp and pathetic. All my usual fight and spirit had deserted me.

'Sarah, they wouldn't touch you. They've not a bit of decency in them, I know, but they wouldn't touch a woman. It's me they were after up at the crossroads. Your name never came into it.'

'I wish I could feel as sure as you do,' I answered, yet part of me thought he was right. I'd never been threatened, and my name hadn't been mentioned. As the weeks passed, I had begun to feel a bit more secure – but then I had thought I would soon be leaving it all behind. Now it was a simple choice. It was Samuel or me. Only one of us could go.

'Would John help me, do you think?' he said quietly.

'Well, I suppose all we can do is ask, but I have no doubt that he will do his best for you if you ask for help.'

'I know he's the one to talk to, Sarah. He seems to know everybody, and I'm sure he will suggest something that we haven't thought of.' He turned to me then, his face grey with worry, and I knew that delay would be dangerous. We had to go immediately. In a flash my mind was made up.

'Go upstairs and pack a bag with enough things for a week or two. I'll go and get the car and check the petrol. Go on right now, get moving,' I warned him, my voice suddenly urgent.

My mind was full of questions as Samuel drove us the twenty miles cross-country to Carrick. How could we organise his escape? If he got to England, how would we keep in touch? Would he be under threat even there?

Maybe he needed to go further afield, to America, where John had many contacts, but the minute the thought entered my mind I dismissed it. I could not let him cross the ocean. It was just too far. I was already scheming, but all the time I assumed it was only for a while until things settled down and the murder was forgotten. I never suspected it would be for a lifetime.

We arrived at Carrick House and pulled up in the yard. I levered myself out of the car and knocked on the kitchen door. The house was in darkness and we waited, listening to the dull signs of movement within.

'Who is it?' John called through the door.

'It's me, Sarah. Samuel's with me,' I said quickly as he leant forward as if to kiss me. He looked over my shoulder, squinting into the darkness.

'Well, you'd better come in,' he said, standing back to let us pass. He was dressed in a long nightshirt and looked faintly ridiculous in the mellow amber light of the hallway. 'What on earth are you doing here at this time of night?'

'We need to talk. It's important.'

He led the way into the kitchen. He opened the door of the stove and riddled the fire to let some heat into the dark shadows of the room.

'Whiskey?' he asked, taking a bottle of Bushmills and three glasses from the cupboard.

'Not for me, thanks, but Samuel could probably do with a drop.'

'Thanks. I will,' Samuel said, and nodded.

'Right, then. You have obviously got some trouble or you wouldn't be here, waking an honest man in the middle of the night. So, are you going to tell me what this is about?'

It all poured out. Between us we went through the details of the loan, the bank calling in the debt that was threatening to ruin us, the row with Hugh and the accidental shooting. Then the tit-for-tat killing of Sean O'Connell and the police investigation.

I had discussed this with John numerous times, as the murders in Lindara were talked about for many weeks. I had been careful to talk only about the facts that were public knowledge, and of course I had never mentioned the part Samuel and I had played in it.

He didn't know that we'd been living in fear these last few weeks, and why should he? He'd had no reason to think that either of us would have had anything to do with the murder. He sat there, unblinking and calm, as we told him the details of it all.

When we had finished, he sat back and looked at Samuel, his eyes intense but his face expressionless.

'I could have told you that Clanhugh was in debt. The old boy had some bad luck with his investments, from what I understand, but the young fellow and that English wife of his … they owed money to all and sundry. I wish I'd warned you about them,' he said, thumping his fist on the table. Samuel and I kept silent.

John was thinking over what he knew about the Clanhughs, and I could see he was blaming himself in part for our misfortune.

'Aw, sure, even if I had warned you, it wouldn't have done any good. You wouldn't have been able to get money out of him that he didn't have. I had no idea that Theo was exposed because of the guarantee. The bank would have insisted on that in the beginning. That's their way. They always have to have the risks covered.'

John lifted the bottle of whiskey and poured himself another drink. He held it towards Samuel, who nodded, and he poured a good measure into his glass as well. Then he carefully diluted Samuel's glass with water from the jug sitting on the table.

'Poor Theo. He would never have allowed this to happen if he'd been in his right mind. Had you any idea of it, Sarah?' he asked, turning to me.

'None at all. My job was running the hotel, and I knew quite a bit about the mill but very little about the UVF. Theo was very careful with information that was confidential. You know how honest he is. He told me little snippets about UVF business but never anything about finances. That was confidential, even from me.'

'Well, it's done now, and there's no undoing it. The money is less important than what we're going to do with you,' he said to Samuel. 'What exactly do you two have in mind?' He looked from me to Samuel and back, waiting for us to explain.

'I think I need to get away,' Samuel said. He paused and glanced at me to see how I was taking it, for he knew I would be left to carry the full burden of Theo and the business on my own. 'It won't be for long. I wouldn't choose to leave Sarah to cope alone. It would just be until things died down and I wasn't under threat any more. Don't think I'm a coward, John. You don't know what it's like to live with the barrel of a gun pointing at you.'

John sighed and sat back from the table.

'The time you should have kept your head was the night of the murder. What possessed you to take off like that and go up to tackle him? You knew he had a temper. You shouldn't have done that, and you shouldn't have taken Sarah with you.'

'But—' Samuel started.

'Look, what's done is done, Samuel,' John interrupted, softer now. 'You don't need to explain to me what it's like. I would hate to be in your position, and I don't envy you one bit.' Then he turned to look at me.

'And what about Sarah? Is she safe, do you think?'

'When they came at me that night, they only threatened me. They didn't mention Sarah. I don't think they have anything against her. I honestly do think you're in the clear, Sarah. I would not leave you otherwise.' I knew what he said was what he honestly believed.

'What do you think, Sarah?' John asked, leaning across the table, searching my face for the answer.

I knew then that I held all our futures in my hand. I had to make the decision for the three of us. Samuel going away wasn't just the simple matter it seemed to him. It was him or me, but he didn't know that. He did not know about John and me, or about the baby, or how in a few weeks' time I had planned to leave Lindara to live in Carrick House. He knew none of this. In his mind I was going to stay in Lindara, and I was not in danger. He just wanted time away to let things calm down and I couldn't blame him for that.

'Samuel and I thought he might go to England for a time … take a new identity, start a new job. We know you have good connections there, and we thought you might be able to arrange it.' I spoke as calmly as I could, but my stomach was churning at the thought of what would happen.

John spoke slowly, for he could see the implications for both of us. I knew his mind was turning over the options as he spoke.

'All that is easily arranged. There is no Liverpool boat on a Sunday night, but we can get the Monday one and be in London by Tuesday dinner time. I can easily make arrangements for a job, lodgings, the lot.'

Samuel's face lit up and he sat up as if a weight was lifted from him.

'That sounds brilliant, John. Thank you.'

'Hold on a minute,' John said firmly. 'Do you realise what you're doing, Samuel?'

Samuel looked at him, half wondering if this was a trick question.

'What do you mean? Of course I know what I'm doing.' John could see that Samuel had his mind set on going, but he wanted him to be fully aware of what it meant.

'If you go, you'll be leaving Sarah with all the problems of your father and the business. You could even be leaving her in some danger. I've heard what you said but she may not be in the clear, even though she hasn't been threatened.'

Samuel hung his head. He wasn't sure what to say, then finally he spoke.

'It'll be hard for Sarah, I know that, but I won't be away for long. It's just until all this calms down.' Then he turned to me and added, 'Get Jean to help you, Sarah. She's good with Dad, and she will make life easier for you.'

John looked from me to Samuel. He was weighing everything up and trying to reach the best decision for everyone.

'Samuel, would you mind giving me and Sarah a minute together? Step outside, there's a good lad.'

John turned to me as the door closed.

'You know what this means, don't you?'

'Only too well,' I blurted out. 'I've thought about nothing else these past few weeks. I knew he would want to go.'

'What do you want to do?'

I looked at John's face and I looked around the kitchen of Carrick, seeing the care he had put into the house in preparation for the baby and me. I knew what it meant to him – possibly even more than it meant to me. The future that both of us had been planning was fading away before our eyes.

'You see, John, if I say no to Samuel and he is killed next week or next month, how would we live with that?'

'I know,' he said, gently pulling me to him and holding me. 'We haven't much choice really, have we?'

I couldn't speak. The tears welled up and burst from my eyes. I couldn't hold in the sobs of bitter disappointment. John stood still, his arms tight around me, giving me strength. He was silent, holding himself in control, managing the depth of his anger. I pulled away from him, wiping the tears from my cheeks with the back of my hands.

'Here,' John said, holding out a linen dishcloth. I wiped my face and splashed water over it from the jug on the table.

'I must be getting back. Theo is on his own and, for once, he has put himself to bed. In fact,' I said, laughing at the picture of him in my mind, 'he was up in bed with all his clothes on, even his boots, tucked in below all the blankets and fast asleep.' We held each other and laughed, slightly hysterically, at the comic image of Theo.

I pulled away from John and went out to the yard, where Samuel was waiting in the dark. I gave Samuel one last hug and he held me tightly, longer than he needed, as if he would never see me again.

'It won't be long, Sarah. Keep well,' were his last words to me.

I turned from him and climbed into the car to make the long journey back to Lindara alone. Now all I had before me was caring for Theo, the problems of the mill and the most immediate question, which was what to do about the baby.

Chapter 25

ROSTREVOR

The two eldest girls came in a pony and trap on the afternoon of the third day and took him away. He was wrapped in a white blanket, and Jane held him while Susan drove the trap. It was near the end of August and the nights were beginning to draw in, so they didn't delay because they wanted to get home before dark. They arrived and were gone again within half an hour.

Nurse Ratcliffe was good to me and I paid her well for her services. It was unusual for her to have a house guest as she usually attended to the needs of the locals in their homes, but she made an exception for me and treated me with kindness and consideration.

'And how are you today, Mrs Brown?' she asked me each morning.

'Oh, on the mend, I think,' I replied, non-committally.

She brought me meals on a tray as I sat by the window, and stopped to say only a few words before leaving me alone. She knew that was what I wanted. I was envious of her house, left to her by a pair of spinster sisters who she had cared for over the years. It sat on a slope overlooking Carlingford Lough and was long and low, with arched ecclesiastical windows set in thick granite walls. It was decorated with muted colours, filled with paintings and books, and at the end of the house there was a sunroom, my favourite place.

Behind the house a meadow ran up to a copse of yellow-green horse chestnuts, then higher up there were blue-green Scots pines and above that the grey granite rocks of the mountains. Looking out across the arc of the bay to the small headland, there were times when it would have been easy to believe I was in Switzerland instead of sitting on the southern shore of County Down.

For the next five days I sat and watched the light on the water of the lough. The sun would come out from behind the clouds and dance across the surface, and then it would suddenly darken as a cloud passed across the sun and the lough would turn from bright sparkling blue to a bleak grey in a matter of seconds. The Mournes lay behind the house, so they never cast a shadow across the steep southern slope. I studied every nuance and movement of light on the water. It was the only chance for peace and solitude in my complicated, crowded life.

On the other side of the lough lay the gentle green slopes of County Meath. In the distance the corn was being cut and harvested. I made out the matchstick figures as they went through the ritual of cutting, drying, tying and stooking. Small boats came and went across the water to Omeath, and black coal boats chugged their way up to the quay at Warrenpoint, trailing a wand of sooty smoke behind them like the fly swat of an African chief.

As I sat there recovering, I imagined I could feel the soft tissues of my body mould back into place, filling the gap left after the birth. I felt the muscles in my stomach relax after months of being held in, defying nature in an attempt to conceal my condition. Now that the baby was gone, I was empty and desolate.

My only consolation was that I knew he would be well cared for. Nurse Ratcliffe sensed some reticence in me, some holding back from my newborn, and she had gently tried to force him on me in those three days after the birth. Although I held him tenderly and looked at his tiny eyes and face and hands, I knew he had to go. My mind had been made up for too long to weaken.

From the moment I set eyes on him I could see he was John through and through. I couldn't resist the wonder of him and, while he slept, I watched him. He was so beautiful, each part of him so tiny and perfect. When he woke, or even sometimes while he slept, I held him in my arms and wallowed in the pleasure of him, his sweet baby smell like new-mown hay.

I would hold him and watch him and breathe in the scent of him. When he opened his eyes, he would fix them on mine and examine me with a long hard unblinking stare, establishing a bond beyond words. My body could not help but respond to his needs and my breasts produced milk in those first three days when he cried to be fed. My heart twisted with each cry and I knew I could have loved him so easily.

I knew I couldn't pass the child off as Theo's. The possibility had, of course, crossed my mind but it wasn't worthy of more than cursory consideration. In the beginning I had tried every means I could think of to get rid of the baby. Gin and hot baths, syrup of figs – I tried them all. Even the more outlandish of old wives' tales were worth a try, but I had the sense to stop short of damaging myself.

The horror of what I was doing finally came to me as I stood on the corner of a small row of red-brick terraces at the end of Sandy Row, looking for the home of an abortionist. I looked at the poor, mean houses and the barefoot, dirty children playing in the street and, as fear and guilt swelled up in me, I made my decision, turned on my heel, and went home. What would be the point of putting my life at risk for the sake of what people might think?

Even then, it was only when I held my baby in my arms and took in the miracle of him that I realised the full consequences of my attempts to destroy him.

At one point I even thought about keeping the baby and brazening it out in Lindara. I didn't really care what the villagers would say.

'Let them talk,' I thought. 'It won't bother me.'

But then I remembered the promise I had made to Theo all those years ago when I'd agreed not to let him down in public, and he in return had given me a free rein to lead the independent life I'd wanted. Now, even though he was in his dotage, I couldn't tarnish his good name. I could have put up with the gossip, but my family would have had to suffer the sniggers and the whispering, and the child would have suffered too in years to come. It was only fair to think of those around me who would be drawn into the mess if I proceeded.

In the end I had to come to terms with the fact of my situation. By then I'd grown used to it, and finally I came to want the baby more than anything. But the murder and its consequences put an end to all that.

Once I knew I was tied to Lindara, the only thing to do was

to find a way to cover up the pregnancy and birth, and have the baby fostered.

In the end John had made me see sense. He arranged it all with the Browns, after making discreet inquiries at the Spa. It was agreed that the two girls would come to Rostrevor for the baby, and John settled the payments for his keep. Violet contacted her sister and made arrangements for Nurse Ratcliffe to take care of me at the birth. She gave her a plausible story about why we couldn't keep the baby with us. It was not unusual in those days for the children of wealthier families to be fostered, and I doubted that it would cause much comment.

After they had taken the baby, I had time on my hands to torture myself with what might have been. Time and again I said to myself,

'If only I had waited.'

Marrying Theo on the rebound as I had, stealing him from Hannah – it all came back to haunt me, now that I couldn't marry the man I wanted. That act of retaliation against Hugh ultimately had only one victim. It saved Hannah from a disastrous marriage to Theo and led her to William, who she was devoted to. It had no impact on Hugh's life. He had never turned a hair when I married Theo. Now, as a result of that decision to pursue Theo all those years ago, I was trapped.

I had committed myself to caring for him, yet there were days when he didn't know me, when I could have been a complete stranger. The truth was that Theo was so far gone in his illness that he could have been cared for by anyone and I was no longer essential to him, but now I was tied to him until his dying day.

With Samuel gone there was no way out. The events of that April night had changed everything. The murder of Hugh, the cover-up that Samuel and I had had to invent, the decision for Samuel to disappear just when the shadows were closing in with their insinuations and their threats … the die had been cast when the shot was fired.

I knew I had to go back to Lindara and carry on as before. I would have the excuse of Samuel's leaving to explain my black moods, my lack of spirit and my need to be on my own. I had struggled long and hard with my conscience and my sense of duty to Theo and to John and our unborn child, but it was all a wasted effort. Just as I could see a way through to the future, just when I'd finally made up my mind about what I should do, events had taken their own course. I was trapped, with no choice but to pick up the pieces and carry on as best I could.

I thought of all the good things I had shared with Theo. He had given me the financial backing to make a success of the hotel and I had learnt so much about business under his tutelage.

I doubted if I would have had the same experience with John. He treated me like a lover – he indulged me, spoilt me, put me on a pedestal – but a part of me knew that I would never have had the equal partnership with John that I'd had with Theo. For that I had to thank Theo.

Sitting there in Rostrevor, recovering from the birth, feeling vulnerable and alone, I just wanted someone to look after me, to care for me. I would have traded all the kindness, money and experience Theo had given me for John's love and protection.

But I would have traded all that again to have been able to keep my son.

CHAPTER 26

WILDERNESS YEARS

I think of that time afterward as the wilderness years. My baby was gone, Samuel was gone, and Theo was more difficult than ever due to his long, slow and inexorable descent into senility. I was tied to the mill and the hotel, working all hours to try and turn around the legacy of debt we now suffered through Hugh's embezzlement of our money. The bank took control of the company but their only interest was in seeing the mill succeed as we employed so many people in the local area. It was a temporary arrangement until we traded our way out of debt and the bank had been fully repaid.

We were lucky to be part of the economic boom immediately after the war ended, from which the whole province benefited. A shortage of food in central and Eastern Europe meant that farm produce almost doubled in price. Demand for flax and linen products escalated, and 1919 was hailed in the papers as the best year ever in the history of the linen industry. Land prices also soared and, with the agreement of the bank and Samuel, I sold some of Theo's acres to help mitigate the debt. Times were hard, but the financial problems kept me focused and gave me a goal. Yet, as time went on, I found it hard to concentrate and stay involved.

My state of mind is recognised now with a proper medical

name, but I knew it then as the nursing sickness – though I would not admit to being ill. Only Violet and I knew about the baby, and she was my strength through the worst of that time. I lived each day with a black cloud over me, and there were many mornings when it was difficult to get out of bed. Violet kept a careful eye on me, gently cajoling me into dealing with my everyday chores. I do not know how I would have coped without her.

My world became the hotel and, when it could not be avoided, the mill. Dixon had taken control of the day to day running of Blackwater Mills and I dreaded the weekly meetings with him. I made excuses not to go, and there were periods when weeks went by without my input. I found reasons to avoid the meetings altogether, and was unable to deal with the deteriorating situation of the disagreements between the workers.

The business was doing well but political animosities had affected the workforce and there were disputes on all sorts of issues, fuelled by the conflict over Ireland's future. The old feisty Sarah would have looked at a problem, assessed it, and then set out a clear strategy for dealing with it, but I could barely even open the reports Dixon sent to me, never mind devise a plan to sort out the problems.

I could have turned to John for help and advice, but it felt wrong to involve him with Theo's business affairs. I had sustained our relationship over the years by keeping the different parts of my life completely separate, and I could not think of giving John access to such private matters. I was too proud to involve my father, and there was no one else I could ask for help. In truth, I was in a deep depression that made me incapable of acting decisively on anything.

I know now that the blackness of my mind was the reason I pushed John away. I could no longer find the energy or will to go anywhere and our meetings became less frequent. A part of me blamed him for the loss of the baby, because it was him who had dealt with the family at the Spa and arranged the fostering. Though I knew he'd done it for me and with my agreement, some part of my heart held him responsible. There was no dramatic final row. We just slowly drifted apart, and I was too low and numb to care.

John travelled a lot at that time, and I heard he was in America half the year on business. When he was home, he worked on Carrick House, pouring his money into the rebuilding and furnishing. I also heard that he was drinking. There were stories of how he went on the binge for days on end, with a gang of young bloods from Portadown who had all inherited a lot of money but little sense. Even then, I couldn't stir myself to feel anything for him. Later, I heard from Ginny there were nights when he never made it home and instead slept the drink off on the couch in her house. When he was in a really bad way, he did not make it beyond the hayshed.

We laid a few people off in the middle of the next year and Teresa O'Connell was first on my list. I remember the nasty smirk on Dixon's face as we agreed that she should be sacked, knowing that he had finally got his way. He was glad to see the back of her, but I was beyond feeling any sense of satisfaction at that time.

The countryside was awash with conflict on both sides of the religious divide. The Easter Rising of 1916 and the end of the war had breathed new life into the Republican cause, while the Ulster Volunteer Force was still active in opposing an independent United Ireland. Men who came home from the war in Europe wanting peace had to take up the fight again on their own home soil, and many of them had little heart for it.

I turned my back on the news, too frustrated to care any more about what was going on. The atmosphere in the village was bleak, with old animosities resurfacing and squabbles breaking out between neighbours. It spilt over into disagreements at the mill, and we would have to separate men who had worked together for years. I tried to be even-handed when we gave men the sack, but Dixon outwitted me. The first casualties were all Catholics. It was not the way I would have run things if I had been in my right mind.

Those years were full of bloodshed and violence, as the various factions fought the bit out over the division of Ireland. The border came into being in May 1921, and it ran across farmland no more than half a mile from the village. The fields we owned to produce flax lay on both sides of the border, and it was not obvious at the start how this would affect us or what impact it would have on the simple logistics of moving the harvest from field to mill.

Workers had to cross over the border and back to get to work, and it just seemed that the whole thing was a solution that created as many problems as it solved. That proved to be the case and 1922 was one of the bloodiest years, with many people killed on both sides. The civil war in the south continued into 1923, but by then things had quietened down in the north. Because I took no notice of the news I was barely aware of the worst of the Troubles even when it was all around me.

Samuel kept in touch, and I made sure he had enough money to continue his education. The Colonel acted as go-between, travelling to England twice a year to take money to him and make sure he was well. Samuel later got a job as a trainee accountant – like his father, he had a great head for figures – but he didn't earn a lot and so family money was always made available to him, even when the mill was not making much money.

He wrote to me under his assumed name, Samuel Orr, and used a poste restante address in London. Knowing that the threat to his life was still very real, we were both still careful to protect his name and whereabouts. He said he was happy there, but he missed Lindara and his job at the mill. Most of all he missed the woods, the countryside and fishing the Blackwater.

Theo was very old and fragile by then. His days of wandering the roads around the village were over, and he never ventured beyond the front door of the hotel. The Colonel kept an eye on him. Even though he appeared to have recovered from the ordeal of the trenches, he was still a vulnerable soul and was very dependent on us. His world was centred on taking care of Theo and providing the coherence and meaning he needed. We could not have asked for more loyalty or devotion from anyone and, in truth, he became a valued part of the family.

Much of the time, Theo slept in a comfortable old chair by the fire in the kitchen, where Violet and the maids could keep an eye on him and look after his needs. He slowly slid towards death, fighting it all the way with a strength of spirit that surprised us. By the end of his life he could no longer get out of bed and we knew it was just a matter of time.

He died on a winter's day in December 1924, and it was truly a relief to me to see the end of his suffering. In the last month of his life I prayed every day that he would be taken. He was a good man who had lived a principled and honest life, and I loved him dearly as a partner and friend.

The morning of the funeral was bitterly cold, with the north-east wind carrying flurries of snow. The church was packed and there were crowds in the churchyard, which did not surprise me because Theo was so well known throughout the whole of the north of Ireland.

As I walked up the aisle behind the coffin to the front of the church, I felt totally alone. Samuel should have been beside me, but he could not come home for the funeral. The feeling across the whole countryside was so bad that his life would certainly have been in peril.

Mother and Father were by my side as we listened to the eulogy and, at the end of the service, Father guided me gently by the arm through the sea of faces and out to the churchyard. As the minister said the ritual words at the graveside and the coffin was lowered into the ground, I felt a deep calm rise through my sadness, knowing that Theo was finally at rest.

It was the Colonel who took it the worst. He stood at the graveside and cried like a child. I moved over and put an arm around him, but the poor fellow could not be consoled.

I moved through the mourners, shaking hands and saying a few words to those I knew. Each one gave me the gift of a kind word or memory.

As I reached the gate of the churchyard, John stepped forward and my heart stopped. I stood for what seemed a lifetime, oblivious of everything around me, aware only of him. I had not seen him for three years and the hard life he had been living was etched on his face, but to me he was as handsome as ever.

I knew then that nothing had changed and that nothing in this world would ever change my love for him. I knew in that instant that I would never let him out of my life again.

'Hello, John,' I said finally.

'Hello, Sarah. Sorry for your trouble.' I wanted to stop right there, to look at him, to put my arms round him and hold him, to talk to him and catch up with the three long years we'd been apart, but I had my duties to carry out.

'You'll come back for a drink?' I said. I saw him hesitate, unsure if I had asked him out of politeness, but before he could refuse, I said, 'You will come back for a drink. I insist.'

I saw the light come into his eyes, and the smile spread across his face as he read my meaning and realised that I was willing to welcome him back.

I turned to take my father's arm for the walk back to the hotel and, even on that cold grey day, I could sense the sun coming out from behind the clouds. I knew that I had turned a corner and that life would only get better from then on.

Chapter 27

CARRICK HOUSE

John went abroad on business shortly after the funeral, but not before we had time to reaffirm our love for each other. The time apart gave me space to mourn Theo and to begin to recover from my depression. The burden of caring for Theo had taken its toll, but after his death the load began to lift from me. It gave me the strength to deal with the mill and to start to take control back from Dixon.

John and I were married at the end of the summer of 1925 and I became mistress of Carrick House. On a fine September morning, he drove me up to the house and carried me over the threshold like a young bride. The house was magnificent. He had restored and extended the house, and furnished it with the best that money could buy.

I went from room to room, taking in the grandeur of the place with new eyes now that it was to be my home. Lindara was only twenty miles away, but it was a world away from the luxury of John's house.

We were both happier than I had ever dreamt possible during those first months. There was so much to rediscover about each other. We entertained friends and family, the house was the talk of the neighbourhood, and Ginny and I became great pals. I realised that any reservations she had had about me in the past were not personal, but were based on concern about John's relationship with a married woman.

It was December when I started to think constantly about our son. As the holiday approached, I could not get him out of my mind. I kept wondering what kind of Christmas our six-year-old boy would have.

'What are we going to do about Jim?' I asked John one morning.

He looked at me in a quizzical way and said,

'What do you want to do about him?'

'I want him back,' I replied without hesitation, but of course it was not quite so simple. How could we explain this child arriving out of the blue? Would we tell the truth? If not, what story would we make up about him? John was as clear-thinking as ever, and suggested that before we made any decisions we should go to the Spa for a visit. The arrangements were made for the following Sunday.

I do not think I was ever as nervous in my life as I was that Sunday afternoon. We drove up the hill from the Spa Hotel, past the golf course to the small wooden bungalow that was the foster family's home.

Ellen was at the front gate waiting for us as we got out of the car. A little face with blonde hair and eyes like saucers appeared over the top of the gate. His gaze was fixed on the car and I could see he was fascinated by it. He was a beautiful lad with a cheeky grin, and he had John's liquid brown eyes.

'Hello, Jim,' I said, smiling at him, but he ran for the cover of Ellen's skirt.

'Just go carefully and take your time,' I told myself. 'You're a stranger to the little lad.'

We sat in Ellen's spartan kitchen as the daughters, Sally and Jane, made tea on the kitchen range. They had everything prepared, and laid out a delicious home-cooked meal in no time. Ellen gave us all the news on wee Jim, as the family called him, and how well he was doing at the village school.

I could see that he was particularly attached to Sally, the youngest daughter. He clung to her, watching us with an earnest unblinking stare, and for all the welcome and the good manners, there was an underlying atmosphere right from the start. I noticed the furtive looks exchanged between the girls when they thought we weren't looking, and I realised that they were dreading having to part with wee Jim. They knew we had come to discuss taking him back with us, but it was the last thing any of them wanted.

As we chatted and drank tea, both John and I tried to talk to Jim, but he was shy of us and would not leave the sanctuary of Sally's lap. Then John leant over to him and said,

'Would you like to see the car, Jim?' That did the trick, and he immediately jumped down and took John by the hand. I watched with tears welling up in my eyes as the two of them, father and son, walked down the garden path.

As we were taking leave of them, John leant down and said to Jim,

'You can come home with us next time and you'll be able to go in the car every day.'

There was a moment's silence. And then the place was in uproar. Jim yelled loudly that he was not going anywhere with us. Sally was bawling, pleading with us not to take wee Jim away. Poor Ellen was looking from us to Sally, totally perplexed, trying to calm the situation down. It was a bad end to the visit.

Neither of us spoke in the car. We watched the headlights catch the outline of the naked winter trees as we sat, as if in two separate bubbles, worlds apart. Both of us were confused, unhappy and searching within ourselves to find the right way forward. I thought of Ellen and her family, the warmth and love inside her house, and how respected she was in the district as the local midwife. We could not have placed Jim with a better foster mother.

John knew when to leave me be and, in the end, it was me who broke the silence.

'I can't do it, John. I cannot take him away from them. They are his family and they are all he has ever known. It wouldn't be right to move him now.'

John sighed loudly, and I knew his dream of raising our son was as important to him as it was to me.

'You see, Ellen is ten times the mother I will ever be. I have been playing at being the businesswoman, the wife, the mistress, while she's been raising a family on a pittance and doing it with love, kindness and wisdom. She's a better person than I will ever be.'

'Aw, now, don't be so hard on yourself, Sarah. You are an excellent businesswoman, and few people would have stood by Theo and Samuel the way you did. You should give yourself credit for that,' John said kindly, and then we lapsed into silence once again.

In the end we decided to leave Jim at the Spa, but when it

was time for him to go to senior school, he would come to live with us and go to school in Armagh.

Life went on for us as before, but there was a cloud over our happiness. It was around that time that I started to think the house was jinxed. Silly little things went wrong with the plumbing, the roof, and with a new kind of decor we tried in the kitchen, which faded and peeled. None of the events were disasters but we got used to local craftsmen being dumbfounded, unable to explain the problems. It was never one big thing, but the accumulation of small problems grated on me.

Over the next few years, I tried to recapture our first months of happiness in the house. I ignored the nagging of my conscience, which told me I would never be happy living on the profits of gunrunning, but somehow it grew in my mind and took hold.

It all came to a head in the summer of 1930, when Jim was eleven and we brought him home to live with us. He was so unhappy that he wrote to Jane and Sally to come and fetch him, so they borrowed a neighbour's car and secretly took him back.

It all sounded such an adventure, such fun to Jim, Jane and Sally, but for John and me it was a nightmare. We had brought Jim home with the best intentions, to do well by him, but he was wild and unkempt, and he had not even the most basic manners. He and I clashed from the start and, even if I chided him gently about his manners, he would speak back to me or run off.

He was awfully headstrong and stubborn, and it was a very unhappy time for both of us. I was not surprised when he ran away, but it was difficult to come to terms with my failure. In the end we had to accept that he wanted to stay with Ellen's family, and we made sure that they were supported financially.

It was after that period of my life that I began to think about leaving Carrick House. Somehow that summer's events with Jim put the final cap on all my misgivings about the place, and I came to the conclusion that we would never find happiness there. I had some money of my own from my part of Theo's will, and I had always had a yen to go back to Lindara.

John took a lot of persuading, but in the end he agreed that if that was what I wanted, he would go with me. I bought a ready-furnished house from a widow, and left Carrick with only my personal possessions. I did not take one single thing with me from that house. I walked out and left behind everything that dirty money had bought. John was torn because it was his pride and joy, but he left Carrick House with me, leaving the decision about what to do with it for another day.

In no time gypsies had broken in and stolen what they could easily carry. John was devastated. We knew that they would break in again if the house was not occupied. The solution was quite simple in the end. John's brother, Fergus, was still farming the land and his young family had grown, so he and his family moved from the cottage into Carrick House. I never for one second regretted leaving that house. It was nothing but a curse to both of us, but it became a happy home for Fergus, his family and the next generations of Browns.

We went back to Lindara and from the day we moved, it was as if everything we had worked for together in life fell into place. Since the outbreak of peace, and at my insistence, John had moved on from his old ways and was now working in the machinery business. He supplied tractors and farm equipment to wealthy farmers. The main part of his business was in factory machinery brought from Belgium, Germany, Italy and America. These were all contacts he had made through his work for the movement, but they were now geared to business, not conflict.

His new business interests blossomed, and we were able to enjoy the wealth that he was making from legitimate commerce. The Colonel came back to work for us soon after we settled in and he became a part of the household. I know people remember him for his foul mouth and crabby ways, but he would do anything for me. Nothing was ever too much trouble for him. He was a gem of a man.

I remember the day Jim knocked on the door. I did not recognise him. He was nineteen and had just bought his first motorbike. He came of his own free will to find his mother and father. I was taken aback at first, and could not hide my surprise, but once I got over the initial shock, I asked him in. That was the beginning of a new phase in our lives, when we acquired a son. It wasn't easy to begin with, but we slowly built a relationship that became strong and solid over time. I got on well with your mother too, and when you were born it was as if you were mine right from the start.

Those were the best years of my life. John and I were blissfully happy together and even the fact that we never had another child did not mar our contentment. We were born to be together, John and me, and in the end, we got to enjoy years of perfect marriage. He died one month after you were born.

How you would have loved him. I see him in you, in your

eyes, in your laugh, and mostly in your calm and wise ways. He would have been so proud of you.

So, what about Samuel? How does he fit into the picture after all these years?

He and I never lost touch. Never. He went to live in London, trained as an accountant, and then some years later took up the post of bursar at one of the Cambridge colleges. He lived there for the rest of his life. John and I visited a few times and he was happy there, but he missed Ireland terribly.

When things were more peaceful, in the period before all the present troubles started, he came and stayed at the lakes in Enniskillen. One day he came to the village and fished on the Blackwater just by the bridge, and I walked over and stopped for a chat as if I was just passing the time of day with a stranger. We did that regularly for years, for they have sharp eyes and long memories in this part of the world and neither of us wanted to risk him being recognised. The O'Connells have never forgotten that one of them was wrongly murdered and Samuel was the cause of it. Nor have they ever forgiven me for firing Teresa from the mill.

So, you see, I could never relax my guard. For all these years I have had to protect Samuel. That is why I never talked much about the family or of times gone by. It was easier to follow the old saying – Whatever you say, say nothing. Better not to get caught up in a web of lies. I have seen that questioning look in your eyes so many times because it was you, more than anyone, who probed into the family history. It was for you that I wrote this.

Poor Samuel never forgave himself for the murder and its terrible consequences on Sean O'Connell's wife, Mary. She was never the same. She had only the one son left when her husband was shot dead, and Samuel did try to repay his debt by leaving Michael his inheritance. It was his final way of making amends for an accident that had weighed on all of them for over fifty years.

In my mind I have relived that night, time and again, and asked if things could have been different. Could I have talked Samuel out of confronting Hugh? Would he have been open to reason?

I see so clearly the moonlit drive on the way to the house, and Samuel's grim face and determined stride … the east wing with the light at the end two windows, Hugh's scowling face when he saw us and Poacher's low growl of greeting. I can recall every detail of the discussion, how it became more heated, Hugh's face getting red and angry, and Samuel trying to keep himself under control. I can see him rising from his chair and turning to the gun cabinet, the glass glinting in the candlelight as it opened, and then confusion, mayhem, as they grappled for control of the gun.

I remember clearly the thoughts that went through my mind – of that cool day of the Pig Tea Party when Hugh brought Lucinda home, of the barefaced lies he had told as a child, of the haughty arrogance of the two of them, of their spendthrift ways in the midst of war and poverty, and of the despicable tone with which he treated Theo. And then, for him to threaten the life of my beloved Samuel was more than I could bear.

As the images reeled through my mind, I could feel the cold metal under my finger and the slightest reflex that pulled the trigger and changed our lives forever. I have relived it a thousand times since that night, wondering if it was a dream. But I could never fool myself. It was me who pulled the trigger.

Would it have done any good to tell Samuel? When he left the inheritance to Michael O'Connell, I realised how much guilt he had lived with for years. I have wondered if it would have eased his mind if I had confessed that it was me who did the deed. But we were both responsible. We both had our hands on the gun, and I am sure that if we had not killed Hugh then Samuel would have been the one who died. He made a good life for himself in Cambridge and there was never a suitable time to discuss it all again.

I left the subject alone and we got on with our lives, but that question has always haunted me.

I was sorry Hugh died – that was never meant to happen – but neither Samuel nor I deserved to spend our life in jail after what Hugh had done to us. It was Sean O'Connell's murder that we both regretted most, but how could we have predicted or prevented it? We could not have foreseen it.

What I do know is that what we did was wrong and cannot be justified for any reason, neither political nor personal, and I have never tried to condone or excuse what happened. Those were the times we lived in then – the lawless wild times of feuding over the division of Ireland – but it still goes on and, indeed, I wonder if it will ever come to an end.

Chapter 28

OLIVIA, 1984

Olivia sipped her coffee and looked down at the endless stretch of the Atlantic far below. She was counting the hours and minutes until touchdown at Logan, where Adam would be waiting for her. Although she had only been in Ireland for one week and they talked every day on the phone, it seemed that they had been apart for ages. Now she could not wait to see him again and to be back in their apartment in the city, with everything that Boston had to offer on the doorstep. It was a life she loved.

When she looked back on how the events in her life had fallen into place, she had often thought that she was destined to meet Adam. The visit to Cambridge to find out about her step-uncle Samuel had been a turning point, and although it could be construed as chance, she'd always felt there was a purpose in it. Her fascination with the city and the university made her wonder why she had never considered studying there. In a conversation with Samuel's friend she had mentioned this, and he'd asked in detail about her degree and if she had any research interests. He then said simply,

'Leave it with me. I will get back to you.'

Within a few days she had an interview at Samuel's old college and was offered a postgraduate course, with a full scholarship that was paid for by the money her uncle had endowed the college with. Samuel's friend had made the introductions and set up the interview, but he assured her that she would not have been selected as the first recipient of the donation if her academic credentials in biochemistry had not been up to scratch. The competition for places at Cambridge was intense and she had got her place on merit.

At the end of the course she had had numerous opportunities, mostly in England, but there was one at Harvard that interested her. She had been torn between that and one in London, but her mind was suddenly made up one evening, almost like the toss of a coin.

She had been having dinner with a university friend, Rosie, and her family in London, including friends of Rosie's parents, two of whom were hereditary Lords. As the evening had progressed the conversation had turned to accents, and to her astonishment the two peers proceeded to discuss how appalled they were that the BBC were now using people with regional accents as presenters. Olivia had remained silent while Rosie squirmed, but she'd winked at her to show she was not upset.

Olivia had been surprised that those who were meant to have the finest manners could be so insensitive, and deliberately so. But it did not offend her, it amused her, and she laughed to herself about it on the way home. She could not and would not be upset by it. It said more about them than it did about her and her Ulster accent, but it made her think she needed to move away from England and its old hierarchies and backward-looking ideas. The decision to move to Boston was made.

She and Adam met on Cape Cod within her first weeks in America. They had been introduced by mutual friends.

The moment their eyes met they both knew the other was special. He was tall and tanned with dark hair and eyes, and she remembered smiling to herself, thinking that he was the perfect example of the well-bred college-educated athletic American. Her estimate of him proved to be correct when she got to know him and his family. He was a student at Harvard and his family were well-off, liberal professionals. It was a stratum of American society that she had grown to know and admire, and she was only too glad to be accepted into their ranks.

Their romance developed quickly, and they had two years of courtship while they finished their education prior to getting married. Now, after the years in America, Olivia knew she would never live in Ireland, or England, again. She also knew that no matter how long she lived in America, or how much she loved the country, she would always be Irish to the core. She still called Ireland home, much to Adam's amusement.

Yet she was always glad to return to Boston, where there were no soldiers patrolling the streets, no bomb threats, no announcement of kneecappings or killings as a regular feature on the daily news. Every time she returned, she wondered how the people in the religious ghettos of Belfast survived the long war of attrition that had no sign of ending.

She knew after university at Queen's that she could not stay in Ireland, and she had decided her life was not going to be lived in a war zone. She had great admiration for those who worked for peace and better understanding between the two communities, who put themselves and their families at risk, but it took a certain kind of commitment and doggedness to do that.

Olivia knew that she didn't have either. There were, in her opinion, too few in Ireland with the spirit of Gandhi and too many with the mentality of Rambo. She lacked the patience to deal with the doublespeak, the twisted arguments, the unwillingness to see the other point of view. She had embraced wholeheartedly the straightforwardness of America, which to her was epitomised by the street signs directing people simply to *WALK* or *DON'T WALK*.

There was no point in allocating blame for the long years of violence – though, in Olivia's mind, no one escaped responsibility. The British had been happy to leave the government of the province to the old power structure that kept the Catholic population without their fair share of jobs, houses and votes. Meanwhile, the Protestant hegemony was happy to rule to its own advantage. The move from civil rights marches to violence on both sides had been easy because no one had mastered the art of negotiation.

The Irish, too, were complicit in the crimes, by allowing military training to take place openly in the countryside along their border and often turning a blind eye to killers on the run. It seemed that no one in that so-called Christian country was without blame.

She glanced down to check that the red leather notebook was safe in her bag. When she had found it in her grandmother's study she had sat down and read it straight through in one sitting. It was late in the evening when she finally finished it, and she knew that the notebook would from then on be one of her most treasured possessions. In years to come she would pass it on to a son or a daughter, but for now she would keep it safe.

Sarah's story had not been out of her thoughts for a moment since she had read the notebook. She turned it over in her mind, again and again, marvelling at how the life of one woman could be so eventful and so rich. The notebook covered events that had happened sixty or seventy years ago, but the issues of loyalty and family chimed with many questions she had grappled with herself. And though Olivia knew the village and the Clanhugh estate from her own childhood, she had never imagined the stories those places could tell. What a life to have lived, and what a secret to take to your grave.

As the plane dipped down to land at Logan Airport, Olivia looked out at the sweep of the bay and the familiar landmarks of Gloucester, Salem and Marblehead. She knew that the sadness she felt at her grandmother's death would fade in time and life would return to normal, but she also knew that some part of her was now complete.

Her life had already been enriched by the contents of one small red leather notebook.

Acknowledgements

Firstly, I must thank Jenny Edwardson, for nagging me for years to get this book finished.

Thanks also to Rosanna Whitehead, for her editing skills and suggestions and to my daughter Julia Breatnach for the journalistic skills she brought to the final edit.

My sister Margaret for reminding me of the story about the colonel and the church women – it was one of the many anecdotes I included which had a real story behind it. Likewise, my cousin George Brown who always amuses me with his memories of our happy childhoods.

Uncle Fergus, sadly deceased, who was the family historian and had an amazing memory. I rang him from Singapore to ask for information about his brother Joe who was captured there. At the age of 86 Uncle Fergus reeled off all the information I asked for and then added Joe's service number, a number I will now never forget.

And to the friends who read the manuscript and gave me encouragement:

Tricia Barnes, Fiona Reynolds, Deborah Wainwright, Daphne McCann, Averil Hawthorne, Helen Walker, Jo Crompton, Liz Jarvis, Freda Brier, Sue McMeeking, Jill Fox, Jan Roberts, Diane Hallas, Kate Newstead, Annie Chambers.

My friends in Adelaide, Australia – Ingrid Fox, Rima Lloyd, Julia Della Flora.

For my very dear friends who helped with early versions of the book but are sadly no longer with us – Noreen Jones and

Liz Howes.

A special thanks to the team at 2QT – Catherine, Karen and Charlotte. You are absolutely brilliant to work with and I really appreciate your expertise and encouragement.

And finally for Peter who has supported and encouraged me all the way.

About the author

Ruth Kirby-Smith grew up in Northern Ireland and studied politics at Queen's University, Belfast during the civil rights era. She completed a Masters in City Planning and worked in Stormont and London. In 1978 she joined a team at Cambridge University undertaking research into the regeneration of the inner city. When her children were born, she took time out and set up a business, designing and selling baby products, which she ran successfully for the next thirty years. Now retired, she lives in Leeds with her husband and enjoys travelling, reading, writing, golf, tennis and spending time with her grandchildren.

Lightning Source UK Ltd.
Milton Keynes UK
UKHW010630090421
381714UK00001B/204